THE COMMITMENTS

Roddy Doyle was born in Dublin in 1958. His first novel, *The Commitments*, was published to great acclaim in 1987 and was made into a very successful film by Alan Parker. *The Snapper* was published in 1990 and has also been made into a film, directed by Stephen Frears. *The Van* was shortlisted for the 1991 Booker Prize and made into a film also by Stephen Frears. *Paddy Clarke Ha Ha Ha*, which won the Booker Prize in 1993, was the largest-selling winner in the history of the prize and has been published in nineteen languages.

BY RODDY DOYLE

Novels

The Commitments
The Snapper
The Van
Paddy Clarke Ha Ha Ha
The Woman Who Walked Into Doors

Plays

Brownbread
War

Roddy Doyle

THE
COMMITMENTS

V

VINTAGE

Published by Vintage 1998

4 6 8 10 9 7 5 3

Thanks to Mick Boland, John Condon, Enda Farrelly, Darren
Gallagher, Louise Hamilton, Caroline Jones, Lorraine Jones,
Kenneth Keegan, Kevin McDonald, Brian McGinn,
Jimmy Murray and Michael Sherlock.

First published in Great Britain by
William Heinemann Ltd 1988

Vintage
Random House, 20 Vauxhall Bridge Road,
London SW1V 2SA

Random House Australia (Pty) Limited
20 Alfred Street, Milsons Point, Sydney
New South Wales 2061, Australia

Random House New Zealand Limited
18 Poland Road, Glenfield, Auckland 10,
New Zealand

Random House (Pty) Limited
Endulini, 5a Jubilee Road, Parktown 2193, South Africa

The Random House Group Limited Reg. No. 954009
www.randomhouse.co.uk

A CIP catalogue record for this book
is available from the British Library

ISBN 0 74 939168 5

Printed and bound in Great Britain by
Cox & Wyman, Reading, Berkshire

**THIS BOOK IS DEDICATED
TO MY MOTHER AND FATHER**

Honour thy parents, Brothers and Sisters.
They were hip to the groove too
once you know. Parents are soul.

Joey The Lips Fagan

ACKNOWLEDGMENTS

When a Man Loves a Woman, words and music by C. Lewis/A. Wright, © 1966 Pronto Music Inc./Quinvy Music Publishing Company; and *Knock on Wood*, words and music by Eddie Floyd/Steve Cropper, © 1966 East Publishers Inc., reproduced by kind permission of Warner Bros Music Limited.

Superbad, words and music by James Brown, © 1970 Crited Music; *Get Up, I Feel Like Being a Sex Machine*, words and music by James Brown/ Bobby Byrd/Ronald L. Lenhoff, © 1970 Dynatone Publishing Co.; and *It's a Man's Man's Man's World*, words and music by James Brown/ Betty Mewsome, © 1966 Dynatone Publishing Co., reproduced by kind permission of Intersong Music Limited.

Out of Sight, words and music by James Brown, and *Night Train*, words and music by Washington/Simpkins/Forrest, reproduced by kind permission of Carlin Music Corp.

Walking in the Rain, words and music by Spector/Mann/Weil, © 1964 Screen Gems–EMI Music Inc., USA, sub-published by Screen Gems– EMI Music Ltd, London WC2H 0LD. Reproduced by permission.

I'll Feel a Whole Lot Better, words and music by Gene Clark, © 1965 Lakeview Music Publishing Co. Limited, 19/20 Poland Street, London W1V 3DD. International Copyright Secured. All Rights Reserved. Used by Permission.

Reach Out I'll Be There, words by B. Holland, L. Dozier, E. Holland, © 1966 Jobete Music Co., Inc, JOBETE MUSIC (UK) LTD. All Rights Reserved. Used by Permission. International Copyright Secured.

What Becomes of the Broken Hearted?, words by P. Riser, J. Dean, W. Weatherspoon, © 1966 Jobete Music Co., Inc, JOBETE MUSIC (UK) LTD. All Rights Reserved. Used by Permission. International Copyright Secured.

Chain Gang, words and music by Sam Cooke, reprinted by permission of ABKCO Music Ltd.

—SOMETIMES I FEEL SO NICE —

GOOD GOD ————
I JUMP BACK ——

I WANNA KISS MYSELF ————!
I GOT —
SOU — OU — OUL —
AN' I'M SUPERBAD ————

James Brown, *Superbad*

—We'll ask Jimmy, said Outspan. —Jimmy'll know.

Jimmy Rabbitte knew his music. He knew his stuff alright. You'd never see Jimmy coming home from town without a new album or a 12-inch or at least a 7-inch single. Jimmy ate Melody Maker and the NME every week and Hot Press every two weeks. He listened to Dave Fanning and John Peel. He even read his sisters' Jackie when there was no one looking. So Jimmy knew his stuff.

The last time Outspan had flicked through Jimmy's records he'd seen names like Microdisney, Eddie and the Hot Rods, Otis Redding, The Screaming Blue Messiahs, Scraping Foetus off the Wheel (—Foetus, said Outspan. —That's the little young fella inside the woman, isn't it?

—Yeah, said Jimmy.

—Aah, that's fuckin' horrible, tha' is.); groups Outspan had never heard of, never mind heard. Jimmy even had albums by Frank Sinatra and The Monkees.

So when Outspan and Derek decided, while Ray was out in the jacks, that their group needed a new direction they both thought of Jimmy. Jimmy knew what was what. Jimmy knew what was new, what

1

was new but wouldn't be for long and what was going to be new. Jimmy had Relax before anyone had heard of Frankie Goes to Hollywood and he'd started slagging them months before anyone realized that they were no good. Jimmy knew his music.

Outspan, Derek and Ray's group, And And And, was three days old; Ray on the Casio and his little sister's glockenspiel, Outspan on his brother's acoustic guitar, Derek on nothing yet but the bass guitar as soon as he'd the money saved.

—Will we tell Ray? Derek asked.

—Abou' Jimmy? Outspan asked back.

—Yeah.

————Better not. Yet annyway.

Outspan was trying to work his thumb in under a sticker, This Guitar Kills Fascists, his brother, an awful hippy, had put on it.

—There's the flush, he said. —He's comin' back. We'll see Jimmy later.

They were in Derek's bedroom.

Ray came back in.

—I was thinkin' there, he said. —I think maybe we should have an exclamation mark, yeh know, after the second And in the name.

—Wha'?

—It'd be And And exclamation mark, righ', And. It'd look deadly on the posters.

Outspan said nothing while he imagined it.

—What's an explanation mark? said Derek.

—Yeh know, said Ray.

He drew a big one in the air.

—Oh yeah, said Derek. —An' where d'yeh want to put it again?

2

—And And,

He drew another one.

—And.

—Is it not supposed to go at the end?

—It should go up his arse, said Outspan, picking away at the sticker.

* * *

Jimmy was already there when Outspan and Derek got to the Pub.

—How's it goin', said Jimmy.

—Howyeh, Jim, said Outspan.

—Howayeh, said Derek.

They got stools and formed a little semicircle at the bar.

—Been ridin' annythin' since I seen yis last? Jimmy asked them.

—No way, said Outspan. —We've been much too busy for tha' sort o' thing. Isn't tha' righ'?

—Yeah, that's righ', said Derek.

—Puttin' the finishin' touches to your album? said Jimmy.

—Puttin' the finishin' touches to our name, said Outspan.

—Wha' are yis now?

—And And exclamation mark, righ'? ——And, said Derek.

Jimmy grinned a sneer.

—Fuck, fuck, exclamation mark, me. I bet I know who thought o' tha'.

—There'll be a little face on the dot, righ', Outspan explained.

3

—An' yeh know the line on the top of it? That's the dot's fringe.

—Black an' whi'e or colour?

—Don't know.

—It's been done before, Jimmy was happy to tell them. —Ska. Madness, The Specials. Little black an' whi'e men. ———I told yis, he hasn't a clue.

———Yeah, said Outspan.

—He owns the synth though, said Derek.

—Does he call tha' fuckin' yoke a synth? said Jimmy.

—Annyway, no one uses them annymore. It's back to basics.

—Just as well, said Outspan. —Cos we've fuck all else.

—Wha' tracks are yis doin'? Jimmy asked.

—Tha' one, Masters and Servants.

—Depeche Mode?

—Yeah.

Outspan was embarrassed. He didn't know why. He didn't mind the song. But Jimmy had a face on him.

—It's good, tha', said Derek. —The words are good, yeh know ———good.

—It's just fuckin' art school stuff, said Jimmy.

That was the killer argument, Outspan knew, although he didn't know what it meant.

Derek did.

—Hang on, Jimmy, he said. —That's not fair now. The Beatles went to art school.

—That's different.

—Me hole it is, said Derek. —An' Roxy Music went to art school an' you have all their albums, so yeh can fuck off with yourself.

4

Jimmy was fighting back a redner.

—I didn't mean it like tha', he said. —It's not the fact tha' they went to fuckin' art school that's wrong with them. It's —(Jimmy was struggling.) —more to do with —(Now he had something.) ——the way their stuff, their songs like, are aimed at gits like themselves. Wankers with funny haircuts. An' rich das.

——An' fuck all else to do all day 'cept prickin' around with synths.

—Tha' sounds like me arse, said Outspan. —But I'm sure you're righ'.

—Wha' else d'yis do?

—Nothin' yet really, said Derek. —Ray wants to do tha' one, Louise. It's easy.

—Human League?

—Yeah.

Jimmy pushed his eyebrows up and whistled.

They agreed with him.

Jimmy spoke. —Why exactly ——d'yis want to be in a group?

—Wha' d'yeh mean? Outspan asked.

He approved of Jimmy's question though. It was getting to what was bothering him, and probably Derek too.

—Why are yis doin' it, buyin' the gear, rehearsin'? Why did yis form the group?

—Well ——

—Money?

—No, said Outspan. —I mean, it'd be nice. But I'm not in it for the money.

—I amn't either, said Derek.

—The chicks?

—Jaysis, Jimmy!

5

—The brassers, yeh know wha' I mean. The gee. Is tha' why?

————No, said Derek.

—The odd ride now an' again would be alrigh' though wouldn't it? said Outspan.

—Ah yeah, said Derek. —But wha' Jimmy's askin' is is tha' the reason we got the group together. To get our hole.

—No way, said Outspan.

—Why then? said Jimmy.

He'd an answer ready for them.

—It's hard to say, said Outspan.

That's what Jimmy had wanted to hear. He jumped in.

—Yis want to be different, isn't tha' it? Yis want to do somethin' with yourselves, isn't tha' it?

—Sort of, said Outspan.

—Yis don't want to end up like (he nodded his head back) —these tossers here. Amn't I righ'?

Jimmy was getting passionate now. The lads enjoyed watching him.

—Yis want to get up there an' shout I'm Outspan fuckin' Foster.

He looked at Derek.

—An' I'm Derek fuckin' Scully, an' I'm not a tosser. Isn't tha' righ'? That's why yis're doin' it. Amn't I righ'?

—I s'pose yeh are, said Outspan.

—Fuckin' sure I am.

—With the odd ride thrown in, said Derek.

They laughed.

Then Jimmy was back on his track again.

—So if yis want to be different what're yis doin' doin' bad versions of other people's poxy songs?

6

That was it. He was right, bang on the nail. They were very impressed. So was Jimmy.

—Wha' should we be doin' then? Outspan asked.

—It's not the other people's songs so much, said Jimmy. —It's which ones yis do.

—What's tha' mean?

—Yeh don't choose the songs cos they're easy. Because fuckin' Ray can play them with two fingers.

—Wha' then? Derek asked.

Jimmy ignored him.

—All tha' mushy shite abou' love an' fields an' meetin' mots in supermarkets an' McDonald's is gone, ou' the fuckin' window. It's dishonest, said Jimmy. — It's bourgeois.

—Fuckin' hell!

—Tha' shite's ou'. Thank Jaysis.

—What's in then? Outspan asked him.

—I'll tell yeh, said Jimmy. —Sex an' politics.

—WHA'?

—Real sex. Not mushy I'll hold your hand till the end o' time stuff. ——Ridin'. Fuckin'. D'yeh know wha' I mean?

—I think so.

—Yeh couldn't say Fuckin' in a song, said Derek.

—Where does the fuckin' politics come into it? Outspan asked.

—Yeh'd never get away with it.

—Real politics, said Jimmy.

—Not in Ireland annyway, said Derek. —Maybe England. But they'd never let us on Top o' the Pops.

—Who the fuck wants to be on Top o' the Pops? said Jimmy.

Jimmy always got genuinely angry whenever Top

7

of the Pops was mentioned although he never missed
it.

—I never heard anyone say it on The Tube either,
said Derek.

—I did, said Outspan. —Your man from what's
their name said it tha' time the mike hit him on the
head.

Derek seemed happier.

Jimmy continued. He went back to sex.

—Believe me, he said. —Holdin' hands is ou'.
Lookin' at the moon, tha' sort o' shite. It's the real
thing now.

He looked at Derek.

—Even in Ireland. ———Look, Frankie Goes To
me arse were shite, righ'?

They nodded.

—But Jaysis, at least they called a blow job a blow
job an' look at all the units they shifted?

—The wha'?

—Records.

They drank.

Then Jimmy spoke. —Rock an' roll is all abou'
ridin'. That's wha' rock an' roll means. Did yis know
tha'? (They didn't.) —Yeah, that's wha' the blackies
in America used to call it. So the time has come to put
the ridin' back into rock an' roll. Tongues, gooters,
boxes, the works. The market's huge.

—Wha' abou' this politics?

—Yeah, politics. ———Not songs abou' Fianna fuckin'
Fail or annythin' like tha'. Real politics. (They weren't
with him.) —Where are yis from? (He answered the
question himself.) —Dublin. (He asked another one.)
—Wha' part o' Dublin? Barrytown. Wha' class are

8

yis? Workin' class. Are yis proud of it? Yeah, yis are.
(Then a practical question.) —Who buys the most
records? The workin' class. Are yis with me? (Not
really.) —Your music should be abou' where you're
from an' the sort o' people yeh come from. ———
Say it once, say it loud, I'm black an' I'm proud.

They looked at him.

—James Brown. Did yis know ———never mind.
He sang tha'. ———An' he made a fuckin' bomb.

They were stunned by what came next.

—The Irish are the niggers of Europe, lads.

They nearly gasped: it was so true.

—An' Dubliners are the niggers of Ireland. The
culchies have fuckin' everythin'. An' the northside
Dubliners are the niggers o' Dublin. ———Say it
loud, I'm black an' I'm proud.

He grinned. He'd impressed himself again.

He'd won them. They couldn't say anything.

—Yis don't want to be called And And exclamation
mark And, do yis? Jimmy asked.

—No way, said Outspan.

—Will yeh manage us, Jimmy? said Derek.

—Yeah, said Jimmy. —I will.

They all smiled.

—Am I in charge? Jimmy asked them.

—Yeah.

—Righ' then, said Jimmy. —Ray isn't in the group
annymore.

This was a shock.

—Why not?

—Well, first we don't need a synth. An' second, I
don't like the cunt.

They laughed.

9

—I never have liked him. I fuckin' hate him to be honest with yis.

————I don't like him much meself, said Outspan.

—He's gone so?

He was gone.

—Wha' sort o'stuff will we be doin'? Derek asked.

—Wha' sort o'music has sex an' politics? Jimmy asked.

—Reggae, said Derek.

—No, not tha'.

—It does.

—Yeah, but we won't be doin' it. We'll leave the reggae to the skinheads an' the spacers.

—Wha' then?

—Soul.

—Soul?

—Soul?

—Soul. Dublin soul.

Outspan laughed. Dublin soul sounded great.

—Another thing, said Jimmy. —Yis aren't And And And annymore.

This was a relief.

—What are we Jimmy?

—The Commitments.

Outspan laughed again.

—That's a rapid name, said Derek.

—Good, old fashioned THE, said Jimmy.

—Dublin soul, said Outspan.

He laughed again.

—Fuckin' deadly.

* * *

10

The day after the formation of The Commitments Jimmy sent an ad into the Hot Press classifieds:

—Have you got Soul? If yes, The World's Hardest Working Band is looking for you. Contact J. Rabbitte, 118, Chestnut Ave., Dublin 21. Rednecks and southsiders need not apply.

★   ★   ★

There was a young guy who worked in the same shop as Jimmy. Declan Cuffe was his name. He seemed like a right prick, although Jimmy didn't know him that well. Jimmy had heard him singing at the last year's Christmas Do. Jimmy had just been out puking but he still remembered it, Declan Cuffe's voice, a real deep growl that scraped against the throat and tongue on its way out. Jimmy would have loved a voice like it.

Jimmy was going to see if he could recruit Declan Cuffe. He took his tray and went over to where he was sitting.

—Sorry, eh ——Declan, said Jimmy. —Is there annyone sittin' here?

Declan Cuffe leaned over the table and studied the chair.

Then he said: —It doesn't look like it.

Normally Jimmy would have upended the slop on the tray over him (or at least would have wanted to) but this was business.

He sat down.

—What's the soup like? he asked.

—Cuntish.

—As usual, wha'.

11

There wasn't an answer. Jimmy tried a different angle.

—What's the curry like?

—Cuntish.

Jimmy changed tactics.

—I'd say yeh did Honours English in school, did yeh?

Declan Cuffe stared across at Jimmy while he sent his cigarette to the side of his mouth.

—You startin' somethin'? he said.

The women from the Information Desk at the table beside them started talking louder.

—Ah, cop on, said Jimmy. —I was only messin'.

He shoved the bowl away and slid the plate nearer to him.

—You were righ' abou' the soup.

He searched the chicken curry.

—Tell us an'annyway. Are yeh in a group these days?

—Am I wha'?

—In a group.

—Doin' wha'?

—Singin'.

—Me! Singin'? Fuck off, will yeh.

—I heard yeh singin', said Jimmy. —You were fuckin' great.

—When did you hear me singin'?

—Christmas.

—Did I sing? At the dinner dance?

—Yeah.

—Fuck, said Declan Cuffe. —No one told me.

—You were deadly.

—I was fuckin' locked, said Declan Cuffe. —Rum an' blacks, yeh know.

12

Jimmy nodded. —I was locked meself.

—I must of had abou' twenty o' them. Your woman, Frances, from the Toys, yeh know her? She was all over me. ——Dirty bitch. She's fuckin' married. ——I sang then?

—Yeah. It was great.

—I was fuckin' locked.

—D'yeh want to be in a group?

—Singin'?

—Yeah.

—Are yeh serious?

—Yeah.

——Okay. ——Serious now?

—Yeah.

—Okay.

★ ★ ★

The next night Jimmy brought Declan Cuffe (by now he was Deco) home from work with him. Deco had a big fry cooked by Jimmy, five slices of bread, two cups of tea, and he fell in love with Sharon, Jimmy's sister, when she came in from work.

—What age is Sharon? Deco asked Jimmy.

They were up in Jimmy's bedroom. Deco was lying on the bottom bunk.

—You're wastin' your time.

—What age is she?

—Twenty, said Jimmy. —But you're wastin' your time.

—I wonder would she fancy goin' out with a pop star.

The door opened. It was the rest of the group,

Outspan and Derek. They smiled when they got in and saw Deco on the bunk. Jimmy had told them about him.

—That's Deco, said Jimmy.

—Howyeh, said Outspan.

—Howyeh, said Deco.

—Pleased to meet yeh, Deco, said Derek.

—Yeah, ——— righ', said Deco.

Deco got up and let Outspan and Derek sit beside him on the bunk.

—How did Ray take the news? Jimmy asked.

—Not too bad, said Derek.

—The cunt, said Jimmy.

—He wasn't too happy with the eh, And And And situation either. Or so he said.

—Yeah. So he said, said Jimmy. —Me arse.

—He's goin' solo.

—He doesn't have much of a fuckin' choice.

They laughed. Deco too.

—Righ' lads, said Jimmy. —Business.

He had his notebook out.

—We have the guitar, bass, vocals, righ'? We need drums, sax, trumpet, keyboards. I threw an ad into Hot Press. Yis owe me forty-five pence, each.

—Ah, here!

—I'll take American Express. ———Now. D'yis remember your man, Jimmy Clifford?

—Tha' fuckin' drip!

—That's him, said Jimmy. —D'yis——

—He was JAMES Clifford.

—Wha'?

—James. He was never Jimmy. What's your name? James Clifford, sir.

14

—Righ', said Jimmy. —James Clifford then. He——

—Tha' bollix ratted on us, d'yis remember? said Derek. —When I stuck the compass up Tracie Quirk's hole. ——They had me da up. Me ma——

—Derek—

—Wha'?

—Fuck up ——Annyway, said Jimmy, —his ma used to make him do piano lessons, remember. He was deadly at it. I met him on the DART there yesterday——

—No way, Jimmy, said Outspan.

—No, hang on, listen. He told me he got fucked ou' o' the folk mass choir. ——D'yis know why? For playin' The Chicken Song on the organ. In the fuckin' church.

—Jaysis!

They laughed. This didn't sound like the James Clifford they'd known and hated.

—Just before the mass, Jimmy continued. —There were oul' ones an' oul' fellas walkin' up the middle, yeh know. An' he starts playin' The fuckin' Chicken Song.

—He sounds okay, said Deco.

No one disagreed with Deco.

—I'll go round to his gaff an' ask him tomorrow, will I?

Outspan and Derek looked at each other.

—Okay, said Outspan.

—So long as he doesn't start rattin' on us again, said Derek. —When we're all gettin' our hole.

—He'll be gettin' his too sure, said Outspan.

—Oh, yeah, said Derek. —That's righ'.

—Does he still wear tha' jumper with the sheep on it?

—They weren't sheep, said Derek. —They were deers.

—They were fuckin' sheep, said Outspan.

—They weren't. ——I should know. I drew a moustache on one o' them.

—Is he workin'? Outspan asked.

—He's a student, said Jimmy.

—Oh, fuck.

—He'll be grand, said Jimmy. —He'll have plenty o' time to rehearse. ——Hang on.

Jimmy put a record on the deck. He'd brought the deck and the speakers up from the front room. He turned to them again.

—D'yis know James Brown, do yis? he asked.

—Was he in our class too? Outspan asked.

They laughed.

—The singer, said Jimmy. —Blackie. He's deadly. ——Did yis see The Blues Brothers?

Outspan and Derek had seen it. Deco hadn't.

—I seen the Furey Brothers, said Deco.

—Fuck off, said Jimmy. —D'yis remember the big woman singer in the coffee place? (They did.) —Tha' was Aretha Franklin. D'yis remember the blind guy in the music shop? (—Yeah.) Tha' was Ray Charles. D'yis remember the preacher in the church? (—No.) --Well, th' was James ——No? (—No.) —In the red cloak? ——The black fella? (—No.) —Yeh have to. ——Derek?

—I don't remember tha' bit.

——Well, tha' was James Brown, said Jimmy. —Hang on ——Rocky IV. Livin' in America, remember? Tha' was him.

—Tha' header!

16

—Yeah.

—Tha' was a shite film, said Derek.

—He was good but, said Jimmy.

—Ah, yeah.

—Annyway, listen to this. It's called Get Up, I Feel Like Being a Sex Machine.

—Hold on there, said Derek. —We can't do tha'. Me ma would fuckin' kill me.

—Wha're yeh on abou'? said Outspan.

—I Feel Like a fuckin' Sex Machine, Derek explained. —She'd break me fuckin' head if I got up an' sang tha'.

—You won't be singin' it, son, said Deco. —I will. An', personally speakin', I don't give a fuck wha' MY ma thinks. ————Let's hear it, Jimmy.

—We won't be doin' this one, Derek, said Jimmy. —I just want yis to hear it, yeh know, just to get an idea, to get the feel o' the thing. ————It's called funk.

—Funk off, said Deco.

Outspan hit him.

Jimmy let the needle down and sat on the back of his legs between the speakers.

—I'm ready to get up and do my thang, said James Brown.

A chorus of men from the same part of the world as James went: —YEAH.

—I want to, James continued, —to get into it, you know. (—YEAH, said the lads in the studio with him.) —Like a, like a sex machine, man (—YEAH YEAH, GO AHEAD.) —movin', doin' it, you know. (— YEAH.) —Can I count it all? (—YEAH YEAH YEAH, went the lads.) —One Two Three Four.

Then the horns started, the same note repeated (—DUH DUH DUH DUH DUH DUH DUH) seven times and then James Brown began to sing. He sang like he spoke, a great voice that he seemed to be holding back, hanging onto because it was dangerous. The lads (in Jimmy's bedroom) smiled at each other. This was it.

—GET UP AH, sang James.

A guitar clicked, like a full stop.

—GET ON UP, someone else sang, no mean voice either.

Then the guitar again.

—GER RUP AH——

Guitar.

—GET ON UP——

—STAY ON THE SCENE, sang James.

—GET ON UP——

James had the good lines.

—LIKE A SEX MACHINE AH——

—GET ON UP——

The lads bounced gently on the bunks.

—YOU GOT TO HAVE THE FEELING——————
    SURE AS YOU'RE BORN AH——————
    GET IT TOGETHER————
    RIGHT ON—
    RIGHT ON————
    GET UP AH, sang James.

—GET ON UP——

Then there was a piano break and at the end of it James went: —HUH. It was the best Huh they'd ever heard. Then the piano got going again.

—GER RUP AH——

—GET ON UP——

18

The guitar clicked away.

And the bass was busy too, padding along. You could actually make it out; notes. This worried Derek a bit. He'd chosen the bass because he'd thought there was nothing to it. There was something to this one. It was busier than all the other instruments.

The song went on. The lads bounced and grinned. Deco concentrated.

—Bobby, James Brown called. (Bobby must have been the man who kept singing GET ON UP.) —Bobby, said James. —Shall I take them to the bridge?

—Go ahead, said Bobby.

—Take 'em all to the bridge.

—Take them to the bridge, said Bobby.

—Shall I take them to the bridge? James asked.

—YEAH, the lads in the studio, and Outspan and Derek, answered.

Then the guitar changed course a bit and stayed that way. James shouted and huh-huhhed a while longer and then it faded out.

Jimmy got up and lifted the needle.

A roar arrived from downstairs.

—Turn down tha' fuckin' radio!

—It's the stereo, Jimmy roared at the floor.

—Don't get snotty with me, son. Just turn it down.

The lads were in stitches laughing, quietly.

—Stupid bollix, said Jimmy. —Wha' did yis think o' tha'?

—Brilliant.

—Fuckin' brilliant.

—Play another one, said Outspan.

—Okay, said Jimmy. —I think yis'll be playin' this one.

19

He put on Night Train for them. It was even more brilliant than Sex Machine.

—We'll change the words a bit to make it — more Dubliny, yeh know, Jimmy told them.

They were really excited now.

—Fuckin' deadly, said Derek. —I'm goin' to get a lend o' the odds for the bass.

—Good man.

—I'd better get a proper guitar, said Outspan. — An electric.

Jimmy played It's a Man's Man's Man's World.

—I'm goin' to get a really good one, said Outspan. —Really fuckin' good.

—Let's go, said Jimmy.

They were off to the Pub.

Deco stood up.

He growled: —ALL ABOARD——
          THE NIGHT TRAIN.

On the way down the stairs they met Sharon coming up.

—Howyeh, Gorgeous, said Deco.

—Go an' shite, said Sharon.

* * *

Jimmy spent twenty minutes looking at his ad in Hot Press the next Thursday. He touched the print. (—J. Rabbitte.) He grinned.

Others must have been looking at it too because when he got home from work his mother told him that two young fellas had been looking for him.

—J. Rabbitte they said.

—That's me alrigh', said Jimmy.

20

—Who d'yeh think yeh are with your J.? Your name's Jimmy.

—It's for business reasons, ma, said Jimmy. —J. sounds better. Yeh never heard of a millionaire bein' called Jimmy.

★ ★ ★

Things were motoring.

James Clifford had said yes. Loads of people called looking for J. Rabbitte over the weekend. Jimmy was interested in two of them: a drummer, Billy Mooney from Raheny, and Dean Fay from Coolock who had a saxophone but admitted that he was only learning how to Make It Talk. There were more callers on Monday. Jimmy liked none of them. He took phone numbers and threw them in the bin.

He judged on one question: influences.

—Who're your influences?

—U2.

—Simple Minds.

—Led Zeppelin.

—No one really.

They were the most common answers. They failed.

—Jethro Tull an' Bachman Turner Overdrive.

Jimmy shut the door on that one without bothering to get the phone number. He didn't even open the door to three of them. A look out his parents' bedroom window at them was enough.

—Who're your influences? he'd asked Billy Mooney.

—Your man, Animal from The Muppets.

Dean Fay had said Clarence Clemons and the guy

21

from Madness. He didn't have the sax long. His uncle had given it to him because he couldn't play it any more himself because one of his lungs had collapsed.

Jimmy was up in his room on Tuesday night putting clean socks on when Jimmy Sr., the da, came in.

—Come 'ere, you, said Jimmy Sr. —Are you sellin' drugs or somethin'?

—I AM NOT, said Jimmy.

—Then why are all these cunts knockin' at the door?

—I'm auditionin'.

—You're wha'?

—Aud-ish-un-in. We're formin' a group. ——A band.

—You?

—Yeah.

Jimmy Sr. laughed.

—Dickie fuckin' Rock.

He started to leave but turned at the door.

—There's a little fucker on a scooter lookin' for yeh downstairs.

When Jimmy got down to the door he saw that his da had been right. It was a little fucker and he had a scooter, a wreck of a yoke. He was leaning on it.

—Yeah? said Jimmy.

—God bless you, Brother J. Rabbitte. In answer to your Hot Press query, yes, I have got soul.

—Wha'?

—And I'm not a redneck or a southsider.

—You're the same age as me fuckin' da!

—You may speak the truth, Brother Rabbitte, but I'm sixteen years younger than B.B. King. And six years younger than James Brown.

—You've heard o' James Brown—

—I jammed with the man.

—FUCK OFF!

—Leicester Mecca, '72. Brother James called me on for Superbad. I couldn't give it my best though because I had a bit of a head cold.

He patted the scooter.

—I'd ridden from Holyhead in the rain. I didn't have a helmet. I didn't have anything. Just Gina.

—Who's she?

—My trumpet. My mentor always advised me to imagine that the mouthpiece was a woman's nipple. I chose Gina Lollabrigida's. A fine woman.

He stared at Jimmy. There wasn't a trace of a grin on him.

—I'm sure you've noticed already, Brother Rabbitte, it was wild advice because if it had been Gina Lollabrigida's nipple I'd have been sucking it, not blowing into it.

Jimmy didn't know what was going on here. He tried to take control of the interview.

—What's your name, pal?

—Joseph Fagan, said the man.

He was bald too, now that he'd taken his helmet off.

—Joey The Lips Fagan, he said.

—Eh ————Come again?

—Joey The Lips Fagan.

—An' I'm Jimmy The Bollix Rabbitte.

—I earned my name for my horn playing, Brother Rabbitte. How did you earn yours?

Jimmy pointed a finger at him.

—Don't get snotty with me, son.

23

—I get snotty with no man.

—Better bleedin' not. ———An' are YOU tryin' to tell me that yeh played with James Brown?

—Among others, Brother.

—Like?

—Have we all night? ———Screaming Jay Hawkins, Big Joe Turner, Martha Reeves, Sam Cooke, poor Sam, Sinatra. ———Never again. The man is a thug. ———Otis Redding, Lord rest his sweet soul, Joe Tex, The Four Tops, Stevie Wonder, Little Stevie then. He was only eleven. A pup. ———More?

—Yeah.

—Let's see. ———Wilson Pickett, Jackie Wilson, Sam an' Dave, Eddie Floyd, Booker T. and the MGs of course, Joe Tex.

—Yeh said him already.

—Twice. Em ———an unusual one, Jimi Hendrix. Although, to be honest with you, I don't think poor Jimi knew I was there. ———Bobby Bland, Isaac Hayes, Al Green.

—You've been fuckin' busy.

—You speak the truth, Brother Rabbitte. And there's more. Blood, Sweat and Tears. The Tremeloes. I know, I know, I have repented. ———Peter Tosh, George Jones, The Stranglers. Nice enough dudes under the leather. I turned up for The Stones on the wrong day. The day after. They were gone.

—Yeh stupid sap, yeh.

—I know. ———Will that do? ———Oh yeah, and The Beatles.

—The Beatles, said Jimmy.

—Money for jam, said Joey The Lips. —ALL YOU

NEED IS LOVE ——DOO DUH DOO DUH
DOO.

—Was tha' you?

—Indeed it was me, Brother. Five pounds, three
and sixpence. A fair whack in those days. ————I
couldn't stand Paul, couldn't take to him. I was up on
the roof for Let It Be. But I stayed well back. I'm not
a very photogenic Brother. I take a shocking photo-
graph.

By now Jimmy was believing Joey The Lips. A
question had to be asked.

—Wha' do yeh want to join US for?

—I'm tired of the road, said Joey The Lips. —I've
come home. And my mammy isn't very well.

Jimmy knew he was being stupid, and cheeky,
asking the next question but he asked it anyway.

—Who're your influences?

—I admit to no influences but God My Lord, said
Joey The Lips. —The Lord blows my trumpet.

—Does he? said Jimmy.

—And the walls come tumbling down.

Joey The Lips explained: —I went on the road nine,
no ten maybe eleven years ago with a gospel outfit,
The Alabama Angels, featuring Sister Julie Bob
Mahony. They brought me to God. I repented, I can
tell you that for nothing, Brother Rabbitte. I used to
be one mother of a sinner. A terrible man. But The
Lord's not a hard man, you know. He doesn't kick up
at the odd drink or a swear word now and again.
Even a Sister, if you treat her with proper respect.

Jimmy had nothing to say yet. Joey The Lips carried
on.

—The Lord told me to come home. Ed Winchell, a

25

Baptist reverend on Lenox Avenue in Harlem, told me. But The Lord told him to tell me. He said he was watching something on TV about the feuding Brothers in Northern Ireland and The Lord told the Reverend Ed that the Irish Brothers had no soul, that they needed some soul. And pretty fucking quick! Ed told me to go back to Ireland and blow some soul into the Irish Brothers. The Brothers wouldn't be shooting the asses off each other if they had soul. So said Ed. I'm not a Baptist myself but I've a lot of time for the Reverend Ed.

Jimmy still had nothing to say.

—Am I in? Joey The Lips asked.

—Fuck, yes, said Jimmy. —Fuckin' sure you're in. ——Are yeh on the phone?

—Jesus on the mainline, said Joey The Lips, —tell him what you want. 463221.

Jimmy took it down.

—I'll be in touch with yeh. Definitely. The lads'll have to see ——to meet yeh.

Joey The Lips threw the leg over his scooter. His helmet was back on.

—All God's chillun got wings, he said, and he took off out the gate, over the path and down the road.

Jimmy was delighted. He knew now that everything was going to be alright. The Commitments were going to be. They had Joey The Lips Fagan. And that man had enough soul for all of them. He had God too.

★   ★   ★

The Commitments used the garage of Joey The

26

Lips' mother's house for meeting and rehearsing. The house was a big one on the Howth Road near Killester and the garage was big too.

When they all got there the first time Joey The Lips had it filled with chairs and rugs. They sat back while Joey The Lips counted them for tea-bag purposes.

—Strong tea, Brothers? he asked.

There wasn't an answer so he threw fifteen bags into the pot.

They were all there, their first time together.

Jimmy Rabbitte; manager.

Outspan Foster; guitar.

Deco Cuffe; vocals.

Derek Scully; bass. (He'd bought one, fourth-hand—he thought it was second—for £60. The amp and cabinet were £40 extra and sounded it. He'd made a deal with his ma. She'd paid for the bass and gear and he had to pay the video rental for the next eighteen months. There were no flies on Derek's ma.)

James Clifford; piano.

Billy Mooney; drums.

Dean Fay; sax.

And Joey The Lips.

This was the first time they'd seen Joey The Lips, and they weren't happy. He looked like a da, their da; small, bald, fat, making tea. He was wearing slippers, checked fluffy ones. One thing made him different though. He was wearing a Jesse Jackson campaign T-shirt.

—Is this the entire band here, Brother Jimmy? Joey The Lips asked.

He was handing out mugs.

—This is it, said Jimmy.

27

—And what have you been listening to? ——You said my man, James Brown, didn't you?

—Yeah, said Jimmy. —We'll be doin' Night Train.

—I like what I hear. ———And?

—Eddie Floyd. Knock On Wood, yeh know.

—Ummm.

—Percy Sledge, said Jimmy.

—When a Man Loves a Woman?

—Yeah.

—Lovely.

—That's all so far really, said Jimmy.

—A good start, said Joey the Lips. —I have some Jaffa Cakes here, Brothers. Soul food.

When they heard that they started to tolerate him. When he took out his trumpet and played Moon River for them they loved him. Jimmy had been annoying them, going on and on about this genius, but now they knew. They were The Commitments.

When they'd finished congratulating Joey The Lips (—Fair play to yeh, Mr Fagan.

—Yeah, tha' was deadly.

—The name's Joey, Brothers.) Jimmy made an announcement.

—I've some backin' vocalists lined up.

—Who?

—Three young ones.

—Young ones. ——Rapid!

—Are they foxy ladies, Jimmy? Joey The Lips asked. They all stared at him.

—Fuckin' sure they are, said Jimmy.

—Who are they? said Outspan.

—Remember Tracie Quirk?

—She's fuckin' married!

—Not her, said Jimmy. —Her sister.

—Wha' one? Derek asked.

—Imelda.

—Wha' one's she? Hang on ————Oh Jaysis, HER! Fuckin' great.

—Which one is it? said Outspan.

—You know her, said Derek. —Yeh fuckin' do. Small, with lovely tits. Yeh know. Black hair, long. Over her eyes.

—Her!

—She's fuckin' gorgeous, said Derek. —Wha' age is she?

—Eighteen.

—She lives beside you, James.

—So I believe, said James.

—Is she anny good at the oul' singin'?

—I haven't a clue, said Jimmy.

—Who're the others? Deco asked.

—Two of her mates.

—That's very good management, Brother, said Joey The Lips. —Will they be dressed in black?

—Yeah ————I ——I think so.

—Good good.

* * *

The time flew in.

Those Commitments still learning their instruments improved. The ones ready were patient. There was no group rehearsing. Jimmy wouldn't allow it. They all had to be ready first.

Derek's fingers were raw. He liked to wallop the strings. That was the way, Jimmy said. Derek found out that you could get away with concentrating on one string. You made up for the lack of variety by thumping the string more often and by taking your hand off the neck and putting it back a lot to make it look like you were involved in complicated work. He carried his bass low, Stranglers style, nearly down at his knees. He didn't have to bend his arms.

Outspan improved too. There'd be no guitar solos, Jimmy said, and that suited Outspan. Jimmy gave him Motown compilations to listen to. Chord changes were scarce. It was just a matter of making yourself loose enough to follow the rhythm.

Outspan was very embarrassed up in his bedroom trying to strum along to the Motown time. But once he stopped looking at himself in the mirror he loosened up. He chugged along with the records, especially The Supremes. Under the energy it was simple.

Then he started using the mirror again. He was thrilled. His plectrum hand danced. Sometimes it was a blur. The hand looked great. The arm hardly budged. The wrist was in charge. He held his guitar high against his chest.

He saved money when he could. He wasn't working but on Saturday mornings he went from door to door in Barrytown selling the frozen chickens that his cousin always managed to rob from H. Williams on Friday nights. That gave him at least a tenner a week to put away. As well as that, he gave the man next door, Mr Hurley, a hand with his video business. This involved keeping about two hundred tapes under his bed and driving around the estate with Mr Hurley for a few hours a couple of times a week, handing out the

30

tapes while Mr Hurley took in the money. Then, out of the blue, his ma gave him most of the month's mickey money. He cried.

He had £145 now. That got him a third-hand electric guitar (the make long forgotten) and a bad amp and cabinet. After that they couldn't get him away from the mirror.

Deco's mother worried about him. He'd be eating his breakfast and then he'd yell something like Good God Y'Awl or Take It To The Bridge Now. Deco was on a strict soul diet: James Brown, Otis Redding, Smokey Robinson and Marvin Gaye. James for the growls, Otis for the moans, Smokey for the whines and Marvin for the whole lot put together, Jimmy said.

Deco sang, shouted, growled, moaned, whined along to the tapes Jimmy had given him. He bollixed his throat every night. It felt like it was being cut from the inside by the time he got to the end of Tracks of My Tears. He liked I Heard It through the Grapevine because the women singing I HEARD IT THROUGH THE GRAPEVINE NOT MUCH LONGER WOULD YOU BE MY BABY gave him a short chance to wet the stinging in his throat. Copying Marvin Gaye meant making his throat sore and then rubbing it in.

He kept going though. He was getting better. It was getting easier. He could feel his throat stretching. It was staying wet longer. He was getting air from further down. He put on Otis Redding and sang My Girl with him when he needed a rest. He finished every session with James Brown. Then he'd lie on the bed till the snot stopped running. He couldn't close his eyes because he'd spin. Deco was taking this thing very seriously.

All his rehearsing was done standing up in front of the wardrobe mirror. He was to look at himself singing, Jimmy said. He was to pretend he had a microphone. At first he jumped around but it was too knackering and it frightened his mother. Jimmy showed him a short video of James Brown doing Papa's Got a Brand New Bag. He couldn't copy James' one-footed shuffle on the bedroom carpet so he practised on the lino in the kitchen when everyone had gone to bed.

He saw the way James Brown dropped to his knees. He didn't hitch his trousers and kneel. He dropped. Deco tried it. He growled SOMETIMES I FEEL SO GOOD I WANNA JUMP BACK AND KISS MYSELF, aimed his knees at the floor and followed them there.

He didn't get up again for a while. He thought he'd knee-capped himself. Jimmy told him that James Brown's trousers were often soaked in blood when he came off-stage. Deco was fucked if his would be.

There was nothing you could teach James Clifford about playing the piano. Jimmy had him listening to Little Richard. He got James to thump the keys with his elbows, fists, heels. James was a third-year medical student so he was able to tell Jimmy the exact, right word for whatever part of his body he was hitting the piano with. He was even able to explain the damage he was doing to himself. He drew the line at the forehead. Jimmy couldn't persuade him to give the piano the odd smack with his forehead. There was too much at stake there. Besides, he wore glasses.

Joey The Lips helped Dean Fay.

—My man, that reed there is a nice lady's nipple.

For days Dean blushed when he wet the reed and let his lips close on it.

—Make it a particular lady, someone real.

Dean chose a young one from across the road. She was in the same class as his brother, third year, and she was always coming over to borrow his books or scab his homework. It didn't work though. Dean couldn't go through with it. She was too real. So the saxophone reed became one of Madonna's nipples and Dean's playing began to get somewhere.

Joey The Lips was a terrific teacher, very patient. He had to be. Even Joey The Lips' mother, who was completely deaf, could sense Dean's playing from the other side of the house.

After three weeks he could go three notes without stopping and he could hold the short notes. Long ones went all over the place. Joey The Lips played alongside him, like a driving instructor. He only shouted once and that was really a cry of fright and pain caused by Dean backing into him while Joey The Lips still had his trumpet in his mouth.

Billy Mooney blammed away at his drums. His father was dead and his brothers were much younger than him so there was no one in the house to tell him to shut the fuck up.

Jimmy told him not to bother too much with cymbals and to use the butts of the sticks as well as the tips. What he was after was a steady, uncomplicated beat: —a thumping backbeat, Jimmy called it. That suited Billy. He'd have been happy with a bin lid and a hammer. And that was what he used when he played

33

along to Dancing in the Streets. Not a bin lid exactly; a tin tray, with a racehorse on it. The horse was worn off after two days.

The three backing vocalists, The Commitmentettes, listened to The Supremes, Martha and the Vandellas, The Ronettes, The Crystals and the The Shangri-las. The Commitmentettes were Imelda Quirk and her friends Natalie Murphy and Bernie McLoughlin.

—How yis move, yeh know ——is more important than how yis sing, Jimmy told them.

—You're a dirty bastard, you are.

Imelda, Natalie and Bernie could sing though. They'd been in the folk mass choir when they were in school but that, they knew now, hadn't really been singing. Jimmy said that real music was sex. They called him a dirty bastard but they were starting to agree with him. And there wasn't much sex in Morning Has Broken or The Lord Is My Shepherd.

Now they were singing along to Stop in the Name of Love and Walking in the Rain and they were enjoying it.

Joined together their voices sounded good, they thought. Jimmy taped them. They were scarlet. They sounded terrible.

—Yis're usin' your noses instead of your mouths, said Jimmy.

—Fuck off slaggin', said Imelda.

—Yis arc, I'm tellin' yeh. An' yis shouldn't be usin' your ordin'y accents either. It's Walking in the Rain, not Walkin' In De Rayen.

—Snobby!

They taped themselves and listened. They got

34

better, clearer, sweeter. Natalie could roar and squeal too. They took down the words and sang by themselves without the records. They only did this though when one of them had a free house.

They moved together, looking down, making sure their feet were going the right way. Soon they didn't have to look down. They wiggled their arses at the dressing table mirror and burst out laughing. But they kept doing it.

* * *

Jimmy got them all together regularly, about twice a week, and made them report. There, always in Joey The Lips' mother's garage, he'd give them a talk. They all enjoyed Jimmy's lectures. So did Jimmy.

They weren't really lectures; more workshops.

—Soul is a double-edged sword, lads, he told them once.

Joey The Lips nodded.

—One edge is escapism.

—What's tha'?

—Fun. ——Gettin' away from it all. Lettin' yourself go. ——Know wha' I mean?

—Gerrup!

Jimmy continued: —An' what's the best type of escapism, Imelda?

—I know wha' you're goin' to say.

—I'd've said that a bracing walk along the sea front was a very acceptable form of escapism, said James Clifford.

They laughed.

—Followed by? Jimmy asked.

35

—Depends which way you were havin' your bracing walk.

—Why?

—Well, if you were goin' in the Dollymount direction you could go all the way and have a ride in the dunes. ———That's wha' you're on abou', isn't it? ——As usual.

—That's righ', said Jimmy. —Soul is a good time.

—There's nothin' good abou' gettin' sand on your knob, said Outspan.

They laughed.

—The rhythm o' soul is the rhythm o' ridin', said Jimmy. —The rhythm o' ridin' is the rhythm o' soul.

—You're a dirty-minded bastard, said Natalie.

—There's more to life than gettin' your hole, Jimmy, said Derek.

—Here here.

—Listen. There's nothin' dirty abou' it, Nat'lie, said Jimmy. —As a matter o'fact it's very clean an' healthy.

—What's healthy abou' gettin' sand on your knob?

—You just like talkin' dirty, said Natalie.

—Nat'lie ——— Nat'lie ——— Nat'lie, said Jimmy. —It depresses me to hear a modern young one talkin' like tha'.

—Dirty talk is dirty talk, said Natalie.

—Here here, said Billy Mooney. —Thank God.

—Soul is sex, Jimmy summarized.

—Well done, Jimmy, said Deco.

—Imelda, said Jimmy. —You're a woman o' the world.

—Don't answer him, 'melda, said Bernie.

36

Jimmy went on. —You've had sexual intercert, haven't yeh?

—Good Jaysis! Rabbitte!

—O' course she has, a good-lookin' girl like tha'.

—Don't answer him.

But Imelda wanted to answer.

—Well, yeah —— I have, yeah. ——So wha'?

There were cheers and blushes.

—Was it one o' them multiple ones, 'melda? Outspan asked. —I seen a yoke abou' them on Channel 4. They sounded deadly.

Derek looked at Imelda.

—Are yeh serious?

He was disappointed in Imelda.

Deco tapped Imelda's shoulder.

—We could make beautiful music, Honey.

—I'd bite your bollix off yeh if yeh went near me, yeh spotty fuck, yeh.

There were cheers.

Imelda ducked her shoulder away from Deco's fingers.

—I might enjoy tha', said Deco.

—I'd make ear-rings ou' o' them, said Imelda.

—You're as bad as they are, 'melda, said Bernie.

—Ah, fuck off, Bernie, will yeh.

—I thought we said slaggin' complexions was barred, said Jimmy. —Apologise.

—There's no need.

—There is.

——Sorry.

—That's okay.

—Spotty.

—Ah here!

Deco grabbed Imelda's shoulders. Bernie was up quick and grabbed his ears.

—Get your hands off o' her, YOU.

—As a glasses wearer, said James, —I'd advise you to carry ou' Bernie's instructions. Yeh might need glasses yourself some day and a workin' set of ears will come in handy.

—That's a doctor gave yeh tha' advice, remember.

Deco took the advice. Bernie gave him his ears back. Imelda blew him a kiss and gave him the fingers.

—Annyway, Imelda, said Jimmy. —Did yeh enjoy it?

—It was alrigh', said Imelda.

More cheers and blushes.

—This lady is the queen of soul, said Joey The Lips.

—Wha' 're you the queen of? Imelda said back.

—Then you agree with us, Jimmy asked Imelda.

—It's oney music, said Imelda.

—No way, 'melda. Soul isn't only music. Soul
——

—That's alrigh' for the blackies, Jimmy. —They've got bigger gooters than us.

—Speak for yourself, pal.

—Go on, Jimmy. ——At least we know tha' Imelda does the business.

—Fuck off, you, said Imelda, but she grinned.

Everyone grinned.

—Yeh said somethin' about a double-edged sword, said James.

—I s'pose the other side is sex too, said Derek.

—Arse bandit country if it's the other side, said Outspan.

—I'm goin' home if it is, said Dean.

—Brothers, Sisters, said Joey The Lips. —Let Brother Jimmy speak. Tell us about the other side of the sword, Jimmy.

They were quiet.

—The first side is sex, righ', said Jimmy. —An' the second one is ————REVOLUTION!

Cheers and clenched fists.

Jimmy went on.

—Soul is the politics o' the people.

—Yeeoow!

—Righ' on, Jimmy.

—Our people. ——Soul is the rhythm o' sex. It's the rhythm o' the factory too. The workin' man's rhythm. Sex an' factory.

—Not the factory I'm in, said Natalie. —There isn't much rhythm in guttin' fish.

She was pleased with the laughter.

—Musical mackerel, wha'.

————Harmonious herring.

—Johnny Ráy, said Dean, and then he roared: — JOHNNY RAY!

—Okay ——Take it easy, said Jimmy.

—Cuntish cod, said Deco.

————Politics. ——Party politics, said Jimmy, — means nothin' to the workin' people. Nothin'. —— Fuck all. Soul is the politics o' the people.

—Start talkin' abou' ridin' again, Jimmy. You're gettin' borin'.

—Politics ——ridin', said Jimmy. —It's the same thing.

—Brother Jimmy speaks the truth, said Joey The Lips.

39

—He speaks through his hole.

—Soul is dynamic. (—So are you.) —It can't be caught. It can't be chained. They could chain the nigger slaves but they couldn't chain their soul.

—Their souls didn't pick the fuckin' cotton though. Did they now?

—Good thinkin'.

—Fuck off a minute. ——Soul is the rhythm o' the people, Jimmy said again. —The Labour Party doesn't have soul. Fianna fuckin' Fail doesn't have soul. The Workers' Party ain't got soul. The Irish people —— no. ——The Dublin people —fuck the rest o' them. ——The people o' Dublin, our people, remember need soul. We've got soul.

—Fuckin' righ' we have.

—The Commitments, lads. We've got it. ——Soul. God told the Reverend Ed ——

—Ah, fuck off.

* * *

They loved Jimmy's lectures. His policy announcements were good too.

—What're they? Derek asked after Jimmy had made one of these announcements.

—Monkey suits, said Jimmy.

—No way, Rabbitte.

—Yes way.

—No fuckin' way, Jim. No way.

—I had one o' them for me mot's debs, said Billy. —It was fuckin' thick. The sleeves were too long, the trunzers were too fuckin' short, there was a stupid fuckin' stripe down ——

40

—I puked on mine at our debs, remember? said Outspan.

—Some of it got on mine too, Derek reminded him.

—Oh, for fuck sake! said Dean. —I'm after rememberin'. ————I forgot to bring mine back. It's under me bed.

—When was your debs? Bernie asked him.

—Two years ago, said Dean.

They started laughing.

—Yeh must owe them hundreds, said Outspan.

—I'd better leave it there so.

—Jimmy, said James. —Are yeh seriously expectin' us to deck ourselves out in monkey suits?

—Yeah. ————Why not?

—Yeh can go an' shite, said Billy.

—Well said.

—Yis have to look good, said Jimmy. —Neat ———— Dignified.

—What's fuckin' dignified abou' dressin' up like a jaysis penguin? Outspan asked.

—I'd be scarleh, said Derek.

Deco said nothing. He liked the idea.

—Brothers, Sisters, said Joey The Lips. —We know that soul is sex. And soul is revolution, yes? So now soul is ————Dignity.

—I don't understand tha', said Dean.

—Soul is lifting yourself up, soul is dusting yourself off, soul is ————

—What's he fuckin' on abou'?

—Just this, Brother. ————Soul is dignity. ———— Dignity, soul. Dignity is respect. ————Self respect. ————Dignity is pride. Dignity, confidence. Dignity,

41

assertion. (Joey The Lips' upstretched index finger moved in time to his argument. They were glued to it.) —Dignity, integrity. Dignity, elegance. —— Dignity, style.

The finger stopped.

—Brothers and Sisters. ——Dignity, dress. —— Dress suits.

—Dignity fuck dignity off dignity Joey.

—Dignity slippers, dignity cardigan.

—Ah, leave Joey alone, said Natalie.

Joey The Lips laughed with them.

Then Jimmy handed out photocopies of a picture of Marvin Gaye, in a monkey suit. That silenced them for a while.

——He's gorgeous, isn't he? said Imelda.

—Yeah, said Natalie.

Joey The Lips looked up from his copy.

—He's up there watching, Brothers.

—Now, said Jimmy when they all had one. — What's wrong with tha'?

—Nothin'.

—He looks grand, doesn't he?

——Yeah.

—We'll get good ones. Fitted. ——Okay?

Outspan looked up.

—Okay.

* * *

One of the best was the night Jimmy gave them their stage names.

—What's wrong with our ordin'y names? Dean wanted to know.

42

—Nothin', Dean, said Jimmy. —Nothin' at all.

—Well then?

—Look, said Jimmy. —Take Joey. He's Joey Fagan, righ'? ——Plain, ordin'ry Joey Fagan. An ordin'ry little bollix.

—That's me, Brother, said Joey The Lips. —I'm the Jesus of Ordinary.

—But when Joey goes on-stage he's Joey The Lips Fagan.

—So?

—He's not ordin'y up there. He's special. ——He needs a new name.

—Soul is dignity, Joey The Lips reminded them.

—What's dignified abou' a stupid name like The fuckin' Lips?

—I bleed, said Joey The Lips.

—Sorry, Joey. Nothin' personal.

Joey The Lips smiled.

—It's part o' the image, said Jimmy. —Like James Brown is the Godfather of Soul.

—He's still just James Brown though.

—Sometimes he's James Mr Please Please Please Brown.

——Is he? said Outspan. —Sounds thick though, doesn't it?

—Ours won't, said Jimmy.

He took out his notebook.

—I've been doin' some thinkin' abou' it.

—Oh fuck!

—Listen. ——Okay, we already have Joey The Lips Fagan, righ'. Now ——James, you'll be James The Soul Surgeon Clifford.

There were cheers and a short burst of clapping.

43

—Is tha' okay? Jimmy asked.

—I like it, said James.

He liked it alright. He was delighted.

—The Soul Surgeon performs transplants on the old piano, he said.

—That's it, said Jimmy. —That's the type o' thing. Everyone in the group becomes a personality.

—Go on, Jimmy.

They were getting excited.

—Derek.

—Yes, Jimmy?

—You're Derek The Meatman Scully.

They laughed.

—Wha' the fuck's tha' abou'? Derek asked.

He was disappointed.

—Are you fuckin' slaggin' me?

—You're a butcher, said Jimmy.

—I know I'm a fuckin' butcher.

—Yeh play the bass like a butcher, said Jimmy.

—Fuckin' thanks!

—It's a compliment, it's a compliment.——Yeh wield the axe, ——know wha'tI mean?

—I'll wield your bollix if yeh don't think of a better name.

—Hang on. —You'll like this. ————Over in America, righ', d'yeh know wha' meat is?

—The same as it is here.

—'cept there's more of it.

—No, listen, said Jimmy. —Meat is slang for your langer.

There were cheers and screams.

—That's fuckin' disgustin', said Natalie.

—Hang on a minute, said Derek. —Is Meatman the

44

American way o' sayin' Langerman?

—Yeah.

—Why not call him Langerman then?

—Or Dickhead, said Deco.

—Fuck off, you, said Derek.

He wasn't happy at all.

—Listen, he said.

This wasn't going to be easy, especially with the girls there.

—There's nothin' special abou' my langer.

—YEEOOW, DEREK!

—Gerrup, Derek, yeh boy yeh!

—A bit of quiet please, Brothers, said Joey The Lips.

—It's the image, said Jimmy. ———Annyway, nobody'll know wha' the name stands for till we break it in the States.

—It's a good name, said Joey The Lips. —Every band needs its Meatman.

———I don't know, said Derek. —Me ma would kill me if she knew I was called after me gooter.

—She won't know.

—I'll tell her, said Outspan.

—Fuck off.

—Righ', said Jimmy. —Next ———Deco.

—Can I be Meatman too, Jimmy?

—No, said Jimmy. —You're Declan Blanketman Cuffe.

—That's a rapid name, said Outspan.

—Politics an' sex, said Jimmy. —Wha' d'yeh think, Deco?

—Yeah, said Deco.

—Billy.

45

—Howyeh.

—Billy The Animal Mooney.

—Ah deadly! Animal. ——Thanks, Jimmy.

—No sweat. ———Okay, Dean next. ——Dean.
Dean sat up.

—You're Dean Good Times Fay.
Cheers.

—That's grand, said Dean.

—Wha' abou' us? said Imelda.

—Hang on, said Jimmy. ——Outspan, we can't call
yeh Outspan.

—Why not?

—It's racialist.

—WHA'!

—It's racialist. ——South African oranges.

—That's fuckin' crazy, Jimmy, said Billy.

—It's me jaysis name, said Outspan.

—Not your real name.

—Even me oul' one calls me Outspan.

—No she doesn't, said Derek.

—Fuck off you or I'll trounce yeh.

—I saw a thing on telly, said Dean. —It said they
make black prisoners, righ', pick the oranges.

—I don't make annyone pick fuckin' oranges! said
Outspan.

—Soul has no skin colour, Brothers and Sisters, said
Joey The Lips.

—I don't even like oranges, said Outspan. ———
'cept them satsumas. ——They're nice.

—Does soul eat oranges, Joey?

—Leave Joey alone, Fuckface, said Jimmy. —Listen,
——your name's Liam, righ'?

—I fuckin' know tha', thanks, said Outspan.

46

—It's not a very soulful name.

—Aah ——fuckin' hell! I can't even have me real name now.

—Shut up a minute. ——What's your second name?

—Wha' d'yeh mean, like?

—I'm James Anthony Rabbitte. What're you?

—Liam, said Outspan.

He went scarlet.

——————Terence Foster.

—Howyeh, Terence, Imelda waved across at him.

He was going to tell her to fuck off but he didn't because he fancied her.

(Along with Jimmy, Derek, Deco, Billy, James and Dean, Outspan was in love with Imelda.)

—Righ', said Jimmy. —You are L. Terence Foster. —Listen to it, said Jimmy. —It sounds great. L. Terence Foster, L. Terence Foster. Doesn't it sound great?

—It sounds deadly, said Derek. —Better than bleedin' Meatman.

—Swap yeh, said Outspan.

—No way, said Jimmy.

—Wha' abou' us? said Bernie.

—Righ', said Jimmy. —Are yis ready, girls? —— Yis are ——Sonya, Sofia an' Tanya, The Commitmentettes.

The girls screamed and then laughed.

—I bags Sonya, said Imelda.

—I'm Sofia then, said Natalie. —Sofia Loren.

—With a head like tha'?

—Fuck yourself, you.

—You've the arse for it anyway, Nat'lie.

47

—Fuck yourself.

—Wha' abou' me? said Bernie.

—She'd forgotten the last name.

—You're Fido, said Deco.

—Fuck yourself, said Natalie.

—Fuck yourself, Deco said back at her.

Natalie spat at his face.

—Here! Stop tha', said Jimmy.

—Hope yeh catch AIDS off it, said Natalie.

Deco let it go because he was in love with Natalie too.

—You're Tanya, Bernie, said Jimmy.

—Why can't I be Bernie?

—It's the image, Bernie.

—You'll always be Bernie to us, Bernie, said James.

—I must say, Jimmy, said Joey The Lips. —You've got a great managerial head on your shoulders.

—Thanks, Joey, said Jimmy.

—Brothers, Sisters, said Joey The Lips. —Would you please put your hands together to show your appreciation to Brother James Anthony Rabbitte.

They clapped, all of them.

★ ★ ★

Then, after months, they were ready to rehearse.

Joey The Lips got rid of some of the chairs to make room in the garage. They had the amps, speakers and mikes in position, and Joey The Lips' mother's upright piano.

They stood around feeling excited but stupid, embarrassed, afraid.

Joey The Lips went around listening to the in-

48

struments. He frowned and turned knobs, listened again, nodded and went on to the next instrument. He impressed the others. Here was a man who knew what he was doing.

Jimmy was lost here. He hadn't a clue how to get the rehearsal started.

Joey The Lips took over.

—Brothers, Sisters. I thank The Lord Jesus for today.

—Fuck off, Joey.

—We'll start with an easy one. Have yaw'l ——

—Yaw'l! For fuck sake!

—Have YOU ALL been listening to What Becomes of the Broken Hearted?

—We sure have, Massa Joey sir boss.

—Whooee!

Joey The Lips played the tape for them. They listened, frightened, to Jimmy Ruffin. They could never do that. Only Deco thought he could do better.

Joey The Lips turned the tape off.

—Alright, Sisters, let's have the Ooh ooh oohs at the beginning.

—God, I'm scarleh, said Imelda.

—Brother James, would you play the girls in please?

—Certainly, Joseph, said James.

Four times James tried to lead the girls but they couldn't follow.

—They're all lookin' at us, said Bernie.

—Hurry up, for Jaysis sake, said Deco.

—No, Declan, said Joey The Lips. —We're in no rush. Rome wasn't built in a day.

—Dublin was though, wha'.

49

—A fuckin' hour.

This time the girls followed James.

—UUH — UUH — UUH

They were shaking. They all heard the shaking in their voices but they didn't look at anybody and kept going.

—UUH — UUH — UUH —

                UUH — UUH — UUH

—That was terrific, ladies, said Joey The Lips. — The Commitmentettes.

—Well done, girls, said Jimmy.

—Right now, said Joey The Lips. —Let's hear The Blanketman.

Deco had the words on a sheet of paper. James donk donk donked, the girls UUH UUH UUHed and then Deco held the mike in his hand and sang. And sang well.

—AS I WALK THIS LAND

  OF BROKE —

               EN DREE — EE — EAMS ———

Deco lifted his voice for single words, then brought it back down again. He stopped before a word (— THIS) and thumped it. He slapped his thigh and tapped the heel of his right foot.

—I HAVE VISIONS O' MANY THING —

                    INGS —

—Sisters, Joey The Lips shouted.

—Wha'? said Natalie.

—I want you to come in there, okay?

—How?

—Joey The Lips sang: —OF MANY THING-INGS. After Declan sings it, okay? ——Right, Brother Deco. ——I have visions.

50

—I HAVE VISIONS O' MANY THING —

                                INGS —

—Sisters!

—OF MANY THINGINGS, sang the girls.

—Good good.

—BUT ——HAPPINESS IS JUST AN ILLU —

                                SHUN —

—Sisters!

—JUST AN ILLUSION —

—Good.

—FILLED WITH SADNESS AN' CON —

                                FEU —

                                SHUN —

—Go with him, girls.

—WHA' BECOMES O' THE BROKE —

                              EN HEARTED —

WHO —

        HAVE LOVES THA' ARE NOW DE-

                          PAR — TED ——

        I KNOW I'VE GOT TO FIND —

        SOME KIND O' PEACE O' MIND ——

        BAY —

                BEEE —

—Right, girls.

—UUH — EEE — UUH.

—Wonderful, Joey The Lips shouted.

He meant it. It had been woeful, but it was a start. Joey The Lips believed in starts. Once you had the start the rest was inevitable. The Lord made sure of that.

It was three in the morning when they stopped. They concentrated on the same song.

There were problems. Joey The Lips spent half the

51

night twiddling knobs and yelling at the rest to get away from the amps. There were shrieks and groans and wails from the speakers.

Billy kept drumming too fast. At half-twelve they found out he'd been messing. Jimmy stepped in and told him off in no uncertain terms. (—You're a cunt, Mooney.) Derek was lost for a while but Joey The Lips told him just to do what James was doing. That was grand, just the same note three times, one and then the other two together, then the same again, and again right through.

The girls were suffering by two o'clock. Joey The Lips had to tune Outspan's guitar for him.

Jimmy had to take Deco aside and tell him to be patient.

—Give them a while, said Jimmy. —They're not ALL naturals.

—I'll try, Jimmy, said Deco. —It's just ——I'm ready, know wha' I mean?

Jimmy nodded.

—There's somethin' in me tryin' to get ou', know wha' I mean?

—I know, said Jimmy. —Take it easy though, okay?

—Okay.

—Fuckin' eejit, said Jimmy. (To himself.)

—Brothers and Sisters, said Joey The Lips at about three. —We have done the good work tonight. Would you all form a circle here, please? You too, Jimmy.

They were too tired to object. They made a circle and, without being told to, held hands.

—Good, said Joey The Lips. —Now drop hands.

They did this.

52

—Turn right.

They did this too. They were still a circle. Each of them was looking at a back. Joey The Lips was in the circle too. He lifted both his hands.

—Now, Brothers, Sisters, we pat ourselves on the back for a job well done.

They laughed as they patted.

* * *

It was the next rehearsal.

—Okay, James, my man, said Joey The Lips. — Take us there.

James looked around. Everyone was at battle stations. He started.

—DUM — DUMDUM —

Joey The Lips pointed to Billy.

—CLAH — CLAHCLAH —

To Derek.

—THUM — THUMTHUM —

Once Derek was in James could be a bit more adventurous. He went along with the girls.

—UUH — UUH — UUH —
      UUH — UUH —
            UUH — UUH — UUH ——

Joey The Lips clicked his fingers. Outspan was off.

—CHI — CHICHI —

Then Deco started to sing.

—AS I WALK THIS LAND
   O' BROKE —
         EN DREE — EE — EAMS ——

It was going well, no mistakes.

Deco would have to be spoken to again. He'd

53

started spinning the mike over his head.

The girls were good. Their step was simple; one step right, then back, then right again. They moved together. And they looked well, about the same height and size. Natalie clapped her hands, shook her head, bared her teeth.

Most of the other Commitments looked comfortable enough.

Dean looked petrified.

—I'LL BE SEARCHIN' EVERYWHERE —
JUST TO FIND SOMEONE TO CARE —
I'VE BEEN LOOKIN' EVERY DAY —
I KNOW I'M GOIN' TO FIND A WAY —
NOTHIN'S GOIN' TO STOP ME NOW —
I WILL FIND A WAY SOMEHOW ———

They all stopped. The record faded quickly there. They didn't know how they were going to end it.

Deco kept singing.

—I'LL SEARCH FOR YOU DOWN ON THE
DOCKS
I'LL WAIT UNDER CLERY'S CLOCK ——

They cheered.

Deco stopped.

—Wha' was tha' abou'? Jimmy asked.

—A bit o' local flavour, said Deco.

—Tha' was deadly, said Derek.

—Yeh said we were goin' to make the words more Dubliny, said Deco.

—It's just ——yeh should've warned us, said Jimmy.

—It's good though, said Billy.

—Very soul, said James.

—Soul is the people's music, said Joey The Lips.

54

—Only culchies shop in Clery's but, said Billy.

—Oh yeah, said Derek. —But, hang on. The clock's hangin' off the outside o' the shop. On the street.

—Soul is street, said Joey The Lips.

—That's alrigh' then, said Jimmy. —The clock stays.

They walked home. Seven of the ten Commitments worked. Four of them made it into work the next morning.

* * *

The Commitments rehearsed three times a week. After the first few nights they stopped before half-eleven for the last bus.

Joey The Lips kept them on the easier, less frantic numbers. Chain Gang became their favourite for a while.

The girls would lift their hammers above their heads, and bring them down:

—HUH ——

And again:

—HAH ——

And again:

—HUH ——

Derek got to sing too.

He'd growl: —WELL DON'T YOU KNOW before Deco sang:

—THAT'S THE SOUND O' THE MEN —
    WORKIN' ON THE CHAIN ——
            GA — EE — ANG ————
THAT'S THE SOUND O' THE MEN —

WORKIN' ON THE —
                              CHAIN GANG ——
Deco closed his eyes a lot for this one.
—ALL DAY THEY'RE SAYIN' —
MY MY MY MY MY MY MY —
                              MY WORK IS SO HARD —
GIVE ME GUINNESS —
I'M THIRSTY ——
MY — Y — Y —
                              MY WORK IS SO HARD —
OH OH MY MY MY —
                              SWEET JAYSIS —
MY WORK IS SO HARD ——
—HUH, went the girls.
—HAH, went the girls.
—HUH, went the girls.
Derek wrapped it up.
—WELL DON'T YOU ——
                              KNOW.

* * *

Joey The Lips had them standing in a circle.
—What're we doin' today, Joey? Dean asked him.
—Well, Brother, said Joey The Lips. —I think
we're going to bring our Soul Sisters to the front.
—Oh Jesus, said Natalie. —I'm scarleh.
—Hang on, said Deco. —What's this?
—The Sisters are going to sing, said Joey The Lips.
—Like the birds of the air.
—They're supposed to be backing vocalists.
—Ah, fuck off, Cuffe, said Billy. —The cunt's
jealous, so he is.

56

—Yeah, said Outspan.

—Sap, said Imelda.

—Grow a pair o' tits, pal, an' then yeh can sing with them, said Billy.

—Are you startin' somethin'?

—Don't annoy me.

—Here! said Jimmy. —None o' tha'.

The time was right for a bit of laying down the law.

—No rows or scraps, righ'.

—Well said, Jim.

—An' annyway, said Jimmy. —The girls are the best lookin' part o' the group.

—Dirty bastard, said Natalie.

—Thanks very much, Jimmy, said Imelda.

—No sweat, 'melda, said Jimmy.

—What'll we sing? Bernie asked Joey The Lips.

—You know Walking in the Rain?

—Lovely.

—I WANT HIM, Imelda sang.

—It doesn't exactly have a strong feminist lyric, does it? said James.

—Soul isn't words, Brother, said Joey The Lips. — Soul is feeling. Soul is getting out of yourself.

—But it's corny.

—You're not singin' it, Specky, said Imelda.

—It's wha' yeh'd call crossover music, Jimmy explained. —It appeals to a wider market. Black an' whi'e. Redneck an' Dub.

—An' it's good, said Natalie.

—You speak the truth, Sister, said Joey The Lips.
———— We need rain and thunder. ——Brother Billy, you can supply us with the meteorological conditions?

—The wha'?

—Rain and thunder?

—I don't know abou' the rain but I can give yeh all the fuckin' thunder yeh want.

He attacked the kit.

—Fuckin' hurricane if yeh want it.

Jimmy spoke. —Can yeh rattle one o' the cymbals gently?

—Gently? ——Jaysis, I don't know. ———How's this?

—Grand, said Jimmy. —That's the rain.

—Good thinkin'.

The girls were practising a move. They crossed their arms over their chests every time they sang HIM.

—The wall of sound. Mr Spector's Wall of Sound here, Brothers, said Joey The Lips. —Brother Outspan, you're the main man on this one.

—Fuck! Am I?

—Stay cool, said Joey The Lips. —Let's hear it.

—CHUNGHA — CHUNGHA — CHUNGHA —CHUNGHA —

—Terrif, said Joey The Lips. —Sisters.

The Commitmentettes got ready.

—Rain, Joey The Lips shouted.

Billy gave him rain.

—Thunder. ———A bit less.

He nodded to the girls.

—DOO DOO DOO DOO DOO —

                              DOOO —

DOO DOO DOO DOO DOO —

                              DOOOooo —

Natalie, in the middle, stepped forward.

58

—I WANT HIM —
—Get up!
—That's not funny, Brother, said Joey The Lips. —
We start again.
—Sorry.
—Rain. ————Now thunder.
—DOO DOO DOO DOO DOO —
                              DOOO —
DOO DOO DOO DOO DOO ——
                              DOOOooo —
I WANT HIM ——
AN' I NEED HIM ——
AN' SOME DAY —
                    SOME WAY —
WOO OH WOO O —
                    O —
                         OH —
                              I'LL SEE HIM —
Bernie and Imelda stepped up to join Natalie. They
sang together now.
—HE'LL BE KIND O' SHY — Y —
Imelda started laughing but they didn't stop.
—AN' REAL GOOD LOOKIN' TOO —
                                   OOO —
AN' I'LL BE CERTAIN —
                         HE'S MY GUY —
COS THE THINGS —
                    HE'LL ——
                         LIKE ——
                              TO ——
                                   DOO ——
—Thunder, Joey The Lips roared.
A cymbal hopped off its stand.

59

—LIKE WALKIN' IN THE RAIN, Natalie sang.

—LIKE WALKIN' IN THE RAIN, Bernie and Imelda sang.

Then they were together again.

—AN' WISHIN' ON THE STARS ——

UP ABOVE —

AN' BEIN' SO —

IN LOVE.

If Outspan had broken one string it wouldn't have mattered. But he broke two so they had to stop till he replaced one of them and Joey The Lips tuned it.

—Tha' was smashin', girls, said Jimmy. —Fair play to yis. They'll be eatin' chips ou' o' your knickers.

—You're fuckin' sick, you are.

* * *

Things were going very well.

There were mistakes, rows, a certain amount of absenteeism but things were going well. Joey The Lips was a calming influence on them. It must have been his age. As well as that, they now knew about his past. They'd seen the photographs of Joey The Lips with the stars:

Joey The Lips and Otis Redding on horses, on Otis' ranch, Joey The Lips said.

Joey The Lips on-stage lying on his back, behind him James Brown's legs, one of them blurred.

Joey The Lips, with hair, in the studio, Gladys Knight, headphoned, smiling at him.

60

Joey The Lips and Marvin Gaye, both in skull caps and caftans, standing in front of a pile of rubble, Detroit.

There was even one of Joey The Lips with B. P. Fallon, Fallon with his arm around Joey The Lips' shoulders, half of Yoko Ono's head in the background.

And Jimmy had found Joey The Lips' name in the credits on a few of his albums. (—Is tha' our Joey? Outspan asked.

—Yep, said Jimmy.

—Fuckin' hell, said Outspan.

He read the list to Derek.

—Berry Gordy, Smokey Robinson, Lamont Dozier, Joey Irish Fagan, Steve Cropper, Martha Reeves, Diana Ross and The Lord, Jehovah. ———— Who's he?) When they saw Joey The Lips looking pleased they knew they were doing alright. And Joey The Lips always looked pleased.

★ ★ ★

Or, Joey The Lips nearly always looked pleased. He looked shocked when Dean found Natalie kissing him.

Dean wasn't looking for them when he found them. He was shutting the garage door and they were behind it. He pulled the door in towards him and there they were, Joey The Lips the one up against the wall, which struck Dean as unusual when he thought about it later. Natalie jumped back, leaving Joey The Lips' right hand holding air. Dean was going to put the door

61

back but Joey The Lips spoke. Natalie had dashed back inside.

—Do I look different? said Joey The Lips.

—No, Joey.

—Good good, said Joey The Lips. —Because you fairly ruffled my savoir faire there, Dean, my man.

—I, said Dean. ———I thought yeh were goin' for chips.

—I am gone, Dean.

If that was a hint or a plea or an order Dean didn't know it because he told the lads when he got back inside. He wasn't ratting. He needed to hear himself saying it. Then he'd be able to believe it.

—FUCK OFF! said Outspan.

—Honest to God, said Dean.

—Where? said Derek.

—Ou' there, said Dean. ——Behind the door.

—It's not fuckin' dark yet.

—I know.

—My Jaysis, wha'!

—Fuckin' hell!

—HEY, YOU! Deco roared across the garage at Natalie.

Natalie was filling the girls in on how she'd got on with Joey The Lips.

—Were you havin' it off with Joey behind the door?

—Fuck yourself.

—Were yeh?

—What's it to you if she was? said Bernie.

—You're fuckin' taller than him! Deco shouted.

This went against nature.

—So?

None of the lads could answer that one. It was ridiculous, but it hurt too. Natalie was a good looking, a lovely looking young one, younger than them. Joey The Lips was a baldy little bollix nearly fifty. He wore slippers ———

For a few minutes The Commitments broke up.

But Jimmy snapped out of it. It happened when he went from the general to the particular. It wasn't Imelda Joey The Lips had got off with. It was Natalie. He didn't fancy Natalie. It was cool.

—It's a free country, lads, said Jimmy.

—God though, said Derek.

—It's not on, said Deco.

He hit the wall, not too hard.

Billy looked from one face to the next for some sign of hope.

—It's like doin' it with your fuckin' da, he said.

—Wha'? said Dean. ——Nat'lie, like? ———Oh, now I get yeh. ———Yeah.

Outspan asked Dean a question.

—Tongues?

—O' course.

—I'm goin' to be sick.

—That's fuckin' cat, tha' is, said Derek.

—Come on, lads, said Jimmy.

He slapped his hands together.

—Cop on, come on. ——Joey's one o' the lads.

—He's a fuckin' oul' fella.

—He's not like other oul' fellas.

—He's exactly like other oul' fellas.

—Do other oul' fellas play in groups? said Jimmy.

—Did your oul' fella play with The Beatles?

63

—My da's got better taste than tha'.

Dean laughed.

—Look, said Jimmy. ———Look. ——He's older than us, righ'. But he's not married, remember. So he's as entitled to move in on a bird as we are. —— An' fair fucks to him.

He meant it.

—Jimmy's righ', men, said James. —It's horrible, but true.

—It's not ——fair though, sure it's not?

—I suppose it's not, said James.

—O' course it's fuckin' fair, said Jimmy. —Look, righ', you could've tried to click with her yourself. But yeh didn't. An' Joey did. So fair fucks to him.

——Still, though, said Derek.

Deco called across to the girls.

—Did he force yeh to? ———Cos if he did ——

The girls screamed laughing.

—Yeh stupid prick, yeh, said Natalie.

—Na'hlie got off with HIM, said Bernie.

They still laughed.

—Why? Outspan asked gently. ——Why, Nat'lie?

—Yeh fuckin' slut! Deco roared.

They all turned on him. Jimmy pointed a finger at him.

—Take it easy.

James and Derek held Outspan back. Dean helped. Outspan stopped struggling. They let him go. Then Outspan jumped at Deco. They pulled him away. He let them. He'd made his point.

James had a psychology exam coming up in a few weeks.

—You moved in on Joey, Nat'lie? he asked.

64

—Yeah. ——I did.

The girls laughed again.

—Yis're disgusted, aren't yis? said Imelda. —She likes him, yis stupid fuckin' saps.

—We all like him, said Outspan. —But we're not queuein' up to get off with him.

They all laughed. Outspan had to think back to see why, but then he grinned.

Natalie grinned.

—No.

She laughed.

—He's nice though. ——He's funny.

—An' he's done all those things, said Bernie.

—That's it! said Deco. —Heh! that's it. She's a fuckin' groupie.

—Well, wha' did you ever do? said Bernie. — Besides wank yourself.

—Bernie! said Imelda.

—Well! —— said Bernie.

—She's a bleedin' groupie. Just cos he ——For fuck sake! ——That's pathe'ic, tha' is.

—You'd get off with Madonna, wouldn't yeh? said Natalie. —Wouldn't yeh? ————Fuckin' sure yeh would.

—She's not behind the garage door too, is she? said Billy.

—Or Joan Collins, said Imelda. —She's fifty.

—Older, said Dean.

—I'd be into Joan in a big way meself, said Jimmy. —I must admit.

—Tina Turner's a granny, said Natalie. —Yeh'd get off with her, wouldn't yeh?

—Well, he got off with his own granny, said Billy.

65

—He might as well have a bash at Tina.

—An' your woman tha' reads the News, said Imelda. —Yeh'd get off with her just cos she reads the News.

—He'd try to get off with Bosco, said Outspan.

When Joey The Lips opened the door they were laughing.

—Soul food, said Joey The Lips.

They stopped laughing and looked awkward, and away from Joey The Lips.

————————Good man, Joey, said Outspan. —I'm fuckin' starvin'. I haven't eaten ann'thin' since me dinner.

Jimmy grabbed Deco's arm.

—Not a word, righ'. Not a fuckin' word, righ'?

Deco freed his arm.

————Righ'.

—You're a randy little bollix all the same, aren't yeh, Joey? said Billy.

They laughed through their shock and embarrassment.

—The soul man's libido, Brother, Joey The Lips explained.

★ ★ ★

By now The Commitments had about a quarter of an hour's worth of songs that they could struggle through without making too many mistakes. They could sound dreadful sometimes but not many of them knew this. They were happy.

Joey The Lips told them that they were ready for

the funkier uptempo numbers, the meaner stuff.

—Rapid!

He didn't say it but Joey The Lips wanted to loosen up Dean, to get him swinging. Dean was the only one still suffering. He stood rigid and even though so far he'd only had three or four note changes at the most per song they usually came too quickly for him and they'd hear him saying Sorry yet again as the rest of them kept going.

A funkier number would force Dean into the open. It would do him good.

Deco was excited. This was where he'd come into his own. He was jumping up and down. He'd started wearing track-suit bottoms during rehearsals. He swallowed teaspoons of honey whenever he wasn't needed for singing.

—Come on, come on, Deco shouted. —Let's go.

—Wha' 're we doin', Joey? Outspan asked.

Jimmy handed the lyrics to the girls and Deco.

—Knock on Wood.

—Deadly!

—I know this one, said Imelda.

—Not the disco version, said Jimmy.

—Aaah!

—No way, said Jimmy. —Use the butt-ends of your sticks for this one, Billy.

—Yes, sir.

They listened to the tape of Eddie Floyd.

—You and me together, Dean, said Joey The Lips.
—Let's show these dudes what a horn section does for a living.

—Jaysis, Joey, I don't know.

Outspan got a chord and hit it.

—THI — THI —

—Is tha' abou' righ', Joey? he asked.

—That's about right. ——Now, Dean, make that baby squeal.

—How?

—We did this one together before.

Joey The Lips put the trumpet to his mouth.

—DUHHH ——

DU —

DUHHH ——

—Remember?

—Oh yeah.

—Good boy. ——Right. ——That's a nipple you've got there.

—Wish it was.

—Ready?

—S'pose so.

—DUHHH ——

DU —

DUH — DEHHH ——

DE —

DEHHH —

—Good good, said Joey The Lips. —And that's where Brother Deco comes in. ——Are we ready, cats?

They were ready.

—A one, a two.

Joey The Lips and Dean blew the intro again.

Billy joined in.

—THU — UNG UNG UNG — THU — UNG UNG UNG —

—I DON'T WANNA LOSE — HUH —

—Stop.

—Why ——What's wrong?

—Brother Deco, said Joey The Lips. —Leave the Huhs till later on, okay. We don't want to alienate our white audience.

—I DON'T WANNA LOSE —

    Outspan: — THI — THI —

THIS GOOD THANG ——

    Billy: —THU — UNG UNG UNG

THA' I'VE GOT ——

IF I DO ——

—DUH DAA DOOHHH, blew Joey The Lips and Dean, very successfully.

—I WOULD SURELY ——

    SURELY LOSE THE LOT ——

Dean wiped his face.

—COS YOUR LOVE —   — THI — THI —

    IS BET HA —   THU — UNG UNG UNG

THAN ANNY LOVE I KNOW — OW —

The Commitmentettes joined in here.

—IT'S LIKE THUNDER —

—DUH UH UHHH, went the horns.

—LIGH' —

            NIN' —

—DEH EH EHHH, went the horns.

—THE WAY YEH LOVE ME IS FRIGH'-NIN' ——

    I'D BET HA KNOCK —

    Billy: THU THU THU THU

—ON WOO — O — OOD —

    BAY —

          BEEE ——

The horns: —DUHHH ——

               DU —

                    DUH — DEHHH ——
                    DE
                         DEHHH —
Dean didn't sleep too well that night.

He'd got through his solo in Knock on Wood.
When they were going through it the third time
before going home Dean had arched his back and
pointed the sax at the ceiling. He'd walloped his
nose but it had been great. He couldn't wait for the
next rehearsal.

                    *   *   *

The Commitments were looser and meaner the next
night, three days later.

—NOW I AIN'T SUPERSTITIOUS, Deco
yelled.

—THI — UH THI, went Outspan's guitar.

—ABOU' YEH —

Billy: —THU — UNGA UNG UNG —

—BUT I CAN'T TAKE NO CHANCE ——

Outspan: —THIDDLE OTHI — UH THI —

—YOU'VE GOT ME SPINNIN' —

    YOU BRASSER ——

    BABY ——

            I'M IN A TRANCE ——

The Commitmentettes lifted their arms and
clicked their fingers while they waited to sing. Derek
bent his knees as he bashed away at his string. Dean
was wearing shades. James hit the keys now and
again with his elbows. Joey The Lips approved and
gave James a thumbs-up. Jimmy grinned and danced
his shoulders.

—IT'S LIKE THUNDER —
The horns: —DUH UH UHHH —
—LIGH' —
          NIN' —
The horns: — DEH EH EHHH —
—IT'S VERY FUCKIN' FRIGH'NIN' ——
    I'D BET HA KNOCK
Billy: —THU THU THU THU
—ON WOO — O — OOD —
    BAY —
          BEEEE ——
The Commitmentettes: —OOOOHH —
The horns: —DUHHH ——
          DU —
               DUH — DEHHH ——
               DE —
                    DEHHH ——

* * *

A week later The Commitments were taking five.
Jimmy was talking to Joey The Lips.
—Have yeh been in any o' the music pubs in town?
—No, said Joey The Lips. —Not my style.
—We prefer somewhere a bit more quieter, don't
we, Joey? said Natalie.
—Behind the garage door, like? said Jimmy.
—Fuck yourself, you.
Natalie went over to Imelda, Bernie and Derek.
Joey The Lips looked straight at Jimmy.
—Rescue me.
—Wha'?
—Rescue me. ——I am a man in need of rescue.

71

—What're yeh on abou'?

Jimmy looked behind him.

—That woman is driving me fucking crazy, said Joey The Lips. —She won't get off my case.

—I think that's the first time I ever heard yeh say Fuckin', Joey.

—She won't leave me alone.

—Well, Jaysis now, Joey, yeh shouldn't of gotten off with her then.

—I had no choice, Brother, Joey The Lips hissed. —She had me pinned to the wall before I could get on my wheels.

—Wha' abou' tha' soul man's ludo yeh were on abou'?

—————What's the smell?

—Wha' smell? ———Hang on.

—Weed, said Joey The Lips.

He looked around, frowning.

—It's hash. ———Here, Jimmy shouted. —Who has the hash?

—Me, said Billy.

Deco, Outspan, Dean and James were with him, over at the piano.

—No way, Billy. ——No way.

—Wha'? said Billy.

The joint, a very amateur job, stopped on the way back to his mouth.

—Hash is out, said Jimmy.

—Why? said Deco.

He was next on it.

—It fucks up your head, said Jimmy.

—Jimmy, said James. —It's been medically proven ———

72

—Fuck off a minute, James, sorry, said Jimmy. —
Yis won't be able to play.

—We'll be able to play better, said Deco.

—It'll wreck your voice.

That shut Deco up while he decided if it was true.

Billy took a long drag and held the joint out for
any takers.

—BLOW THA' OU', BILLY, Jimmy roared.

Billy exhaled.

—I'd die if I didn't, yeh fuckin' eejit.

He still held the joint up in his fingers.

—What's wrong with it? Outspan asked.

Jimmy was doing some thinking. What had
annoyed him at first was the fact that they hadn't got
the go-ahead from him before they'd lit up. He needed
a better reason than that.

—For one thing, he said. —Righ' ——Yis're barely
able to play your instruments when yis have your
heads on yis.

—Ah here!

—Are you sayin' I can't sing, son?

—Second, said Jimmy. ——We're a soul group.
Remember tha'. Not a pop group or a punk group,
or a fuckin' hippy group. ——We're a soul group.

—Wha' d'yeh mean, WE'RE? said Deco.

—Fuck up, you.

Jimmy was grateful for the interruption. It gave
him more time to think of something.

—If you're not happy with the way I'm doin' things
then ——

—We love yeh, Jimmy. Keep goin'.

—Righ'. ——Where was I? ——Yeah. ——We're
a soul group. We want to make a few bob but we

73

have our principles. It's not just the money. It's politics too, remember. We're supposed to be bringin' soul to Dublin. We can't do tha' an' smoke hash at the same time.

—It's oney hash.

—The tip o' the fuckin' iceberg, Billy. Dublin's fucked up with drugs. Drugs aren't soul.

—Wha' abou' drinkin'?

—That's different, said Jimmy. —That's okay. The workin' class have always had their few scoops.

—Guinness is soul food, said Joey The Lips.

—That's me arse, Jimmy, said Outspan.

—Listen, said Jimmy. —For fuck sake, we can't say we're playin' the people's music if we're messin' around with drugs. We should be against drugs. Anti drugs. Heroin an' tha'.

—Yeah, but ——

—Look wha' happened to Derek's brother.

—Leave my brother ou' o' this, said Derek.
He nearly shouted it.

—Okay, sorry. But yeh know wha' I mean.

—Wha' happened to Derek's brother? Billy asked.

—Forget it.

—Wha' happened your brother?

—Forget it, Billy.

—I was oney askin'.

—Annyway, said Jimmy. —Do yis agree with me?

—Ah yeah ——o' course, oney ——

—We'll get a Heroin Kills banner for behind the drums, said Jimmy.

—Hang on, said Deco. —Wha' abou' the niggers in America, the real soul fellas, wha' abou' them? They all smoke hash. ——Worse.

74

This was Joey The Lips' field.

—Not true, Brother. Real Soul Brothers say No to the weed. All drugs. ——Soul says No.

—Wha' abou' Marvin Gaye?

—Wha' abou' him? said Jimmy.

—He died of an overdose.

—His da shot him, yeh fuckin' sap.

—A bullet overdose, said Billy.

—Sam Cooke then, said Deco.

—I don't know wha' happened him. ——Joey?

—Died under very mysterious circumstances, said Joey The Lips. —A lady.

—Enough said.

—I'm sure he was lookin' for it, said Imelda.

—Phil Lynott, said Deco.

—Fuck off, said Jimmy. —He wasn't soul.

—He was black.

—Ah, fuck off an' don't annoy me. ——Get ou' o' my life. ——Annyway, do yis agree abou' the hash? An' the heroin, like?

—Yeah

They all nodded or stayed quiet.

—Can we smoke it after the rehearsal, Jimmy? Billy asked.

—Yeah, sure. No problem.

* * *

It was another week later.

James was late so Joey The Lips was going to put Deco through a new song, James Brown's Out of Sight.

—You're sure you know it now?

75

---O' course I'm sure.

—Okay then. Off you go. ——A one ——

Deco put his hands to his ears.

Outspan nudged Derek.

—Fuckin' tosser.

Deco sang.

—YOU GOT YOUR HIGH HEELED SNEAKERS ON ——

YOUR STUFF IS NEW ——

YOU GOT YOUR HIGH HEELED SNEAKERS ON —

SIMON HARTS —

YOUR GEAR IS NEW ———

YOU'RE MORE THAN ALRIGH — HI — HIGH' ——

YEH KNOW —

YOU'RE OU' O' SIGH' ——Fuck!

Jimmy had come in and made it obvious he wanted The Commitments to notice him when he threw an empty 7-up can at Deco's head.

—Wha' was tha' for? Deco shouted.

—I don't like yeh, said Jimmy. —An' I've a bit o' news for yis.

—So yeh hit ME?

—It didn't hurt, an' neither will me bit o' news.

—Ooh! said Imelda. —Sounds good.

—It is, 'melda, it is indeed. An' you're lookin' lovely tonigh'.

—Thank you, Jimmy. An' you're lookin' horrible as ever.

—The news, said Joey The Lips.

—Are we goin' to have The Angelus first or somethin'? said Outspan.

76

James came in.

—Sorry. ——Puncture.

—Jimmy's got news, James, said Bernie.

—But he's keepin' it to himself, said Imelda. (And she sang this bit.) —BECAUSE HE'S A BOLLIX.

—Are yis ready?

—Ah stop, Jimmy.

—Well, I've been busy for the last couple o' nights.

—Yeh dirty man, said Deco.

Billy thumped him.

—I've been negotiatin', said Jimmy.

—Janey!

—That'll make yeh deaf.

They laughed, but only for a little while.

—I've got us a venue for our first gig.

—Fuckin' great!

There were cheers and grins.

—When?

—Tomorrow week.

—Fuckin' hell!

—It has to be then, said Jimmy. —Because the bingo caller ——yeh know Hopalong ——him, he's goin' into hospital for the weekend to get a tap put into his kidneys or somethin', so it's the only nigh' the place is free.

—The community centre?

—Yeah.

—Tha' kip!

—From little acorns, Brothers and Sisters, said Joey The Lips.

—Barrytown Square Garden, wha', said Outspan.

—Hang on, said Derek. —No slaggin'. It'll do for a start.——Thanks, Jimmy.

—Yeah. Thanks, Jim.

—No sweat.

—We bring the music to the people, said Joey The Lips. —We go to them. We go to their community centre. That's soul.

—No one goes there, Joey, said Outspan. —'cept the oul' ones tha' play the bingo.

—An' the soccer. They change there, said Derek. —An' the operetta society, an' the Vinny de Paul.

—An' Hopalong, said Natalie.

—He's stickin' it into your woman from the shop, Colette, did yis know tha'?

—He is NOT, said Bernie.

—He fuckin' is.

—Good Jesus, that's disgustin'.

—No wonder he limps, wha'.

—Our first gig, said Dean. ———Our first gig.

—Who did yeh have to talk to abou' the hall, Jimmy? James asked.

—Father Molloy.

—Oh fuck! Father Paddy, said Outspan. —The singin' priest, he explained to the lads who weren't from Barrytown.

Derek began to sing.

—MOR —
    NIN' HAS —
        BROKE —
            EN —
    LIKE THE FIRST MOR —
        HOR — HOR — NIN' —
    BLACK BIRD ON —
        TREE TOP —
    HAS HAD ITS FIRST CRAP —

—The folk mass, Outspan explained to the lads. —
Fuckin' desperate.

—Oh yeah, said Billy. —Is tha' the one you got
flung ou' of?

—That's it, said James.

—Did he brown yeh, Jimmy? Outspan asked.

—No. He just ran his fingers through me curly fellas.

—Aah!! Stop tha'! said Natalie.

—How much is it goin' to cost? Deco asked.

—Nothin'.

—That's super.

—How come?

—I told him it was part o' the Anti-Heroin
Campaign.

—Yeh fuckin' chancer, yeh.

They all stood back and admired Jimmy.

—Well, it is, said Jimmy. —We'll have our Heroin
Kills banner. Me little brother, Darren ——he's an
awful little prick ——he's goin' to do it in school. An
art project, like. An' a few posters for the walls an'
things.

—Good man, Jimmy.

—There's one thing but, said Jimmy. —I told
Father Molloy we'd do a folk mass for him.

—No way!

—Only messin'. ——Northside News are sendin'
someone ou' to see us. An' a photographer.

—How come?

—I told them abou' it. Phoned them up.

—Jaysis, fair play to yeh.

—I'll be scarleh, said Bernie.

—I haven't saved enough for me suit, said Derek.

—We can hire them for this one, said Jimmy. —

79

We'll get the bread back on the door.

—Bread! said Billy. —Yeh fuckin' hippy.

—Fuck up.

—Well, Brothers and Sisters, said Joey The Lips. —Let's hear it for our manager, Brother J. Rabbitte, and let's hear it for Brother Hopalong's kidneys too.

The Commitments clapped.

—Brother Hopalong's kidneys are soul.

* * *

The Commitments rehearsed every night of the last week. They began to shout and throw the head when someone made a mistake and they had to start all over again. But Joey The Lips kept them short of panic stations. He said Stay Cool a lot during the week.

—Stay cool, my man, said Joey The Lips.

Deco had just roared at Billy who had just knocked over the snare drum.

—He's a fuckin' eejit, Joey, Deco shouted.

—Joey, said Billy. —I said it before, it's one o' the risks yis have to take. It's part o' me style. These sort o' accidents are likely to happen. I told yis tha'.

He now addressed Deco.

—An' here, you, George Michael. If yeh ever call me a fuckin' eejit again you'll go home with a drumstick up your hole. The one yeh don't sing ou' of.

He started to pick up the drum.

—The one yeh talk ou' of.

—That'll be the day, pal.

—It's comin'. I'm tellin' yeh.

—Maybe.

—Yeh'd want to have your vaseline with yeh the

—Good good.

—Wha' do you know abou' it? said Outspan.

—Fuck all, said Jimmy. —But I got an honour in science in me Inter.

* * *

Deco had bought his suit. He bought the shirt and bow on the Thursday before the gig. The other Commitments managed to get into town to hire their suits.

Joey The Lips got one of his dress suits dry-cleaned. Dean crawled in under his bed and found the one he'd flung under there. He soaked the jacket till the muck was nearly all gone. Then he brought it down to the cleaners.

Black shoes were polished or bought or borrowed.

* * *

Friday was a dress rehearsal.

Joey The Lips was already dressed when The Commitments got there.

—Oh my Jaysis, Joey, wha'! said Outspan.

—Yeh look like Dickie Davis, said Dean.

—I don't know the dude, said Joey The Lips. — But I accept the compliment. Thank you, Brother.

—Yeh look gorgeous, Joey, said Imelda.

—Joey? said Outspan. —How do yeh get your hankie to go like tha'? I can't get mine like tha'.

Joey The Lips let the girls into the kitchen to change. The lads changed in the garage. There was a lot of slagging of underpants and so on. None of them played football so it was a good while since they'd dressed in this way. They enjoyed it.

83

—Jaysis, look at those skid marks.

—Fuck off.

—Come here till I ride yeh, yeh lovely young fella, yeh.

—Fuck off, will yeh.

—Where's it gone? said Outspan.

—Wha'?

—Me knob. ——I could've sworn I tucked it into me sock before I came ou'.

James joined in the crack too.

—Do yeh know wha' the Latin is for tha' weapon yeh have on yeh there?

The small door to the kitchen was knocked.

—Can we come in? Imelda asked.

The lads cheered, and thumped and kicked each other.

Deco cupped his crotch in both hands (although one could have done) and roared: —I've a bugle here yeh can blow on, 'melda.

—Fuck yourself, Natalie roared.

—Jaysis, Cuffe, take it easy. For fuck sake!

—I've an arse here yeh can kiss, Imelda shouted back from behind the door. —Can we come in?

—No.

—Enter, Sisters.

—Well, we're comin'.

Deco cheered.

Imelda was first (—Good fuck!), then Natalie (—Fair fuckin' play to yis, girls), then Bernie.

—I'm scarleh, said Bernie.

The girls were stunning; very tight black skirts to just above the knee with an extension at the back so they could walk, black sleeveless tops, hair held up, except the fringe, as near to the Ronettes as they could

84

manage, black high heels, loads of black eye shadow, very red lipstick.

They were blushing.

Joey The Lips applauded.

Jimmy spoke. —Well, as James says, It don't mean nothin' without a woman or a girl.

—I never said tha', said James.

—James Brown, yeh dick.

The girls admired the suits. There was lots of giggling and redners.

Joey The Lips did their breast pocket hankies for them.

One of Billy's trouser legs was longer than the other.

—Ah, fuck tha', he said.

He looked very disappointed.

—You'll be behind the drums.

—They'll still see me legs.

—I'll fix it up for yeh tomorrow, said Natalie.

—Will yeh? —Thanks.

They played better in the suits. They were more careful, and considerate. Deco's suit seemed to pin him more to one spot. This was good. In his track-suit he hopped around the garage and got in the way and on the nerves. Dean swapped jackets with Jimmy. (—Why have you got a suit? Outspan asked Jimmy.

—Soul is dignity, said Jimmy.

—This is a great fuckin' group, said Outspan. —I must say. Even the skivvies wear fuckin' monkey suits.

—I'm no skivvy, said Jimmy. —I'm your fuckin' manager, pal.

—An' don't you forget it, said James.

—Fuckin' righ', said Jimmy.) There was more room in Jimmy's jacket so Dean could still lift the sax up high. Billy didn't knock over any drums.

Joey The Lips showed Jimmy how to use the mixer.

—So all I have to do is push these lads up or down a bit when the sound's a bit gammy?

—That's correct, said Joey The Lips.

—That's great, said Jimmy. —There's nothin' to it. Anny fuckin' dope could do tha'. I might even pull a few birds this way, wha'. Wha' d'yeh think? Blind them with science, wha'.

—It works, my man. ——It works.

They finished early, got back into their civvies, and went for a drink.

* * *

Kick-off was at half-seven.

The Commitments said they'd meet at the hall at six. Jimmy was there at five, his dress suit hidden by a snorkel jacket he hadn't worn since he'd left school.

Billy arrived soon after with Dean. Billy had his van from work. They got the gear out but they left Joey The Lips' mother's piano in the van until some more arrived to help them.

At half-five the caretaker appeared out of a door beside the stage.

—Wha' do youse want? the caretaker asked.

He saw the drums.

—That's not the bingo stuff.

—There's no bingo tonigh', pal, said Jimmy.

—It's Sahurday but, said the caretaker.

He took his Press out of his jacket pocket and looked at the date.

—Yeah. ———Sahurday.

Jimmy explained. —Hopa ——The fella tha' calls the numbers is in hospital so Father Molloy said we could have the hall for the nigh'.

—He told me nothin' abou' it, said the caretaker. —So yis can take your bongos off o' the stage there an' the rest o' your tackle with it an' get ou'. As far as I'm concerned there's bingo tonigh'. Until I'm officially told otherwise.

—Why don't yeh go across an' ask him? said Jimmy.

Father Molloy's house was right across the road.

—I will not, said the caretaker. —It's not my job to go across an' ask him.

—Wha' is your job? Billy asked.

—I'm the caretaker, said the caretaker.

—You're not very good at it, are yeh? said Billy. —The state o' the place.

—Shut up a minute, Billy, said Jimmy. —Look. ——If I go across to Father Molloy will tha' do?

—Yis'll have to get your gear ou' first. I want nothin' in here till I'm officially informed.

Jimmy looked at Billy and Dean.

They started to gather the drums.

—It's our church collection money goes to pay your wages, Billy told the caretaker.

—I wouldn't get very far on the money you'd put in the collection, so I wouldn't, said the caretaker.

—Well, yeh'll be gettin' tenpence less from now on.

—Make tha' twenty, said Dean.

—That's no problem, said the caretaker. —I put in fifty meself. I'll oney put in thirty from now on.

They were beginning to like each other. The caretaker carried two mike stands for them.

—It's a cushy one, I'd say, is it? said Billy.

—Wha'?

—Your job.

—Oh, it is alrigh', the caretaker admitted. —I do fuck all to be honest with yeh. I watch a few women polishin' the floor on Tuesdays. An' I put ou' the chairs for the bingo. An' I open the windows to get rid o' the smell o' the footballers. That's abou' it. ——Mind you, the pay's useless.

—I s'pose so, said Billy.

He took a cigarette from the packet the caretaker held out.

—The soccer fellas are much smellier than the gaelic ones, said the caretaker. —I think it's because the soccer mammies don't wash their gear as much.

—The gaelic mas would all be culchies, said Dean. —They're always washin' clothes.

—That's very true, said the caretaker. —Will yis be wantin' the chairs ou'?

—No, said Billy. —It's stand-up.

—That'll be great, said the caretaker. —I'll sneak home for Jim'll Fix It. Yis'll be alrigh' by yourselves for a while.

Jimmy came back.

—Father Molloy says it's alrigh'.

—That's great, said the caretaker. —I'll give yis a hand to bring your stuff back in. ——D'yeh think I could have a go on the drums?

88

—No problem.

—I'll show yeh me saxophone, said Dean.

—Oh lovely.

The rest of The Commitments began to arrive.

Joey The Lips and Bernie arrived together, holding hands. Bernie had a crash helmet.

—What's the fuckin' story there? Outspan asked.

—Mind your own business, you, said Imelda.

—Tha' chap's a little rabbit, said Outspan.

—Wha' would you know abou' it? said Natalie.

—I was thinking there, Brother Jimmy, said Joey The Lips.

The girls were in the caretaker's room, changing. The caretaker had gone off home. The lads were sitting or shuffling around the stage, excited, nervous and uncomfortable.

—We need the hard men, bouncers.

—That's all organized, said Jimmy.

—How? Derek asked.

—Mickah Wallace is goin' to do the door for us.

—Oh, good fuck! said Outspan.

He had a small scar on his forehead, courtesy of Mickah Wallace.

—Tha' cunt! He'll fuck off with the money.

—He won't, said Jimmy. —Mickah's alrigh'.

—He's a fuckin' savage, said Derek.

—Who is he? said Deco.

—Wha' is he, yeh mean, said Outspan.

—He got fucked ou' o' our school, righ', Derek told them, —because he beat the shi'e ou' o' the Dean o' Girls. ——Girls! He kicked her up an' down the yard when she snared him smokin' an' she tried to take the pack off o' him.

89

—See tha'?

Outspan thought he was pointing to his scar but his finger was on the wrong side.

—He done tha'. Fucked a rock at me durin' a match. He was the goalie an' I oney had him to beat, the cunt. An' he fucked the rock at me.

—Jaysis!

—I still scored though.

—Yeh didn't, said Derek.

—I fuckin' did.

—Yeh were offside.

—I fuckin' wasn't.

—Fuck up, youse, said Jimmy. —Tha' was years ago. We were all fuckin' eejits then.

Outspan wasn't finished yet.

—He got up on the roof o' Mountjoy when he was in there cos the other guy in his cell had AIDS an' he thrun slates down at the screws.

—That's not true, said Jimmy.

—It is.

—Yeh just said it was him.

Jimmy explained to the rest.

—It was on the News. Some tossers up on the roof. An' Outspan just said one o' them was Mickah.

—I recognized him.

—They had their jumpers wrapped round their faces.

—I recognized his jumper.

—Fuck off. ——He's doin' bouncer an' that's it. He'll be grand.

—Who else? Derek asked.

—We won't need annyone else, said Jimmy. —Nobody's goin' to act the prick with Mickah here.

90

James spoke. —Mickah's okay.

—How would you know?

—I meet him a lot. ——He lent me a few books.

—Yeh still read Ladybird books, do yeh? said
Outspan.

—Don't let Mickah hear yeh sayin' tha', said
Jimmy.

—Let us tune up, Brothers, said Joey The Lips.

The girls came out.

—Yis rides, yis, said Deco.

He stuck his tongue out at them and jiggled it.

—Fuck yourself, said Natalie.

The male Commitments changed.

It was seven o'clock. The caretaker came back.

—Suits, he said.

—Yeah, said Jimmy.

—Monkey suits.

—D'you approve?

—Oh, very nice. It's a long, long time since I seen a
band all dressed the same.

He went over to the girls.

—I know your daddy, he said to Imelda.

—So? said Imelda.

She raised her eyes to heaven.

—You're just like him, said the caretaker. —A
cheeky little fucker.

Mickah Wallace arrived.

—How's it goin', Mickah, said Outspan.

—Alrigh', said Mickah. —An' yourself?

—Alrigh'.

—Guitar, wha'.

—Yeah.

—Are yis anny good?

91

—Alrigh'.

—The best, said Jimmy.

The ones not from Barrytown studied Mickah. He wasn't what they'd expected; some huge animal, a skinhead or a muttonhead, possibly both. This Mickah was small and wiry, very mobile. Even when he was standing still he was moving.

—I haven't a bad little voice meself, yeh know, Mickah told Jimmy. —Give us tha', please, pal.

He took Deco's mike. Deco stood back.

—Don't worry, said Mickah. —Your job's safe.

He bashed the mike into his forehead.

—That's a good strong mike, tha'. Quality's very rare these days.

He tapped the mike.

—Testin' one two, testin'. Time now, ladies an' gentlemen, plea-ese.

He tapped again.

—An' it's Ben Nevis comin' in on the stand side, Lester's ou' o' the saddle. Come on, Ben Nevis, come on, come on. ——Shi'e! He's fallen over an' croaked.

They were afraid to laugh.

—Now I'll sing for yis.

He coughed.

—RED RED —

WIY —

YUN ——

STAY CLOSE TO —

ME —

EE YEAH ——

Wha' comes after tha'?

He gave the mike back to Deco.

92

—Howyeh, James, he said. —Did yeh read tha' one
I gave yeh?

—I'm halfway through it.

—It's better than Catch 22, isn't it?

—I don't think so, Mickah.

—Fuckin' sure it is, said Mickah. —How much in,
Jimmy?

—Two lids.

—Tha' all? Yis mustn't be anny good.

—Time will tell, Brother, said Joey The Lips.

—It told on you annyway, pal, said Mickah.

He was noticing Joey The Lips for the first time.

—The fuckin' state of yeh.

Imelda laughed.

Bernie stared her out of it.

—Can we come in?

A small boy stood at the door.

—No, Mickah shouted down to him.

—When?

—When I say so. Now shut the fuckin' door.

Mickah jumped off the stage. He landed in front of
the caretaker, back in a clean shirt.

—I need a table, son, said Mickah.

Mickah and the caretaker took the table to the door.
They sat behind it. Jimmy drew the stage curtain, a
manky red thing. The Commitments took turns at
peeking through it into the hall. The caretaker got an
empty tin for the money.

—Righ', said Mickah.

He slipped down in his chair and stretched so he
could swing the door open with his foot.

—Get in here, he shouted.

There were about twelve of them outside, all kids,

93

brothers and sisters of The Commitments, and their friends.

The caretaker took the money. Mickah laid down the rules as each of them passed the table into the hall.

—Anny messin' an' I'll kill yeh, righ'.

—I've oney a pound, said one boy.

The caretaker looked to Mickah.

—Let him in, said Mickah.

Jimmy was standing behind them.

—How long are yis on for? Mickah asked him.

—Abou' an hour.

—I'll throw him ou' after half, said Mickah.

—I'm unwaged, said another boy with his pound held out.

—Yeh weren't this mornin' when yeh were deliverin' the milk, said Mickah.

—He sacked me after you seen me.

—Go on.

The caretaker took the pound.

It wasn't a big hall but three hundred could have stood in it. There was room for two hundred and seventy more at half-seven.

Mickah looked outside.

—There's no more ou' there.

Jimmy looked at the crowd. Four mates of himself, Outspan and Derek leaned against the back wall. He'd let them in for nothing. Ray Ward (ex And And! And) was with them. He'd paid in. There were six other older ones, in their late teens or early twenties, mates, he supposed, of Deco or Billy or Dean. There were three girls, pals of Imelda, Natalie and Bernie. The rest were kids, except for one, Outspan's mother. The caretaker got her a chair and she sat at the front, at the side.

Outspan looked again. He dropped the curtain.

—Fuck her, he said. —She promised me she wouldn't come.

—I'm scarleh for yeh, said Bernie.

—Soul has no age limits, said Joey The Lips.

—Fuck off, Joey, said Outspan.

—She's wearin' her fur, Imelda told them.

She was at the curtain.

—Fuck her annyway, said Outspan. —I'm not goin' on.

—If yeh don't go on, said Deco, —I'll tell your pal, Mickah.

Outspan looked at him.

—My ma could beat the shi'e ou' o' Mickah Wallace anny day.

At ten to eight Jimmy shut the door. The numbers had risen by three, his brother Darren and his mates.

Jimmy grabbed Darren's shoulder.

—Come here, you, bollox. There's only one E in Heroin.

He thumped Darren's ear.

—Make them all go up to the front, Mickah, will yeh. It'll look better.

—Righto. ——That's good thinkin'.

—We don't want the group demoralized.

—Fuck, no.

Mickah went along the back. He shoved everyone forward.

—Get up there an clap or I'll fuckin' crease yis.

He was obeyed. Mickah followed them.

—Cheer when the curtain opens, righ'. ——An' clap like fuck. Great gig, Missis Foster, he shouted to Outspan's mother.

Billy stood back and looked at the banner.

—That's not how yeh spell heroin.

Imelda looked at it.

—Oh, look it, she said. —That's brilliant.

—The syringe is very good though, isn't it? said Dean.

—It'll do, said Derek. —It's grand. ——None o' those cunts ou' there knows how to spell an'annyway.

Jimmy was back-stage.

—If we do tha' dance in Walkin' In The Rain we'll fall off the fuckin' stage, said Natalie. —It's much smaller than Joey's garage.

—Yis'll be alrigh', said Jimmy. —You're professionals.

—Janey!

The Commitments were all at their positions.

Jimmy stood at the side of the stage. He had a mike in one hand and the curtain cord in the other. He nodded to them. They looked at themselves and each other and stood, ready, very serious.

This was it. Even if there were only thirty-three in the hall. James Brown had played to less. Joey The Lips said so.

—Ladies an' gentlemen, Jimmy said to the mike.

There was a cheer, a big one too, from the other side of the curtain.

—Will yeh please put your workin' class hands together for your heroes. The Saviours o' Soul, The Hardest Workin' Band in the World, ——Yes, Yes, Yes, Yes ——The Commitments.

He dropped the mike and pulled the cord. The curtain stayed shut.

—Wrong rope, son, said the caretaker.

—Yeh fuckin' sap, said Imelda.

The caretaker got the curtain open. There was another cheer. (Jimmy dashed down to the mixing desk. —Get away from tha', youse.) The house lights were still on. The crowd wasn't even two deep in some places. The caretaker went to turn off the lights.

The clapping stopped. The lights went off. There were a few cheers, but no music.

—Hurry up, a boy shouted.

—Who said tha'? said Mickah. —Which one o' yis said tha'? They watched him tearing along the front, grabbing shoulders.

—Billy, said Joey The Lips.

—Yeah?

—I Thank You.

—Wha'? ——Oh fuck, yeah! Sorry.

—THUH THUH — DAH THUH — THUH THUH — DAH THUH —

THUH THUH — DAH THUH — THUH THUH — DAH THUH —

Deco stepped up and walked along the front of the stage. He looked down at his audience.

—I want everybody to get up off o' your seats an' (—Wha' fuckin' seats? Mickah shouted.) —an' get your arms together an' your hands together an' give me some o' tha' Ooold Soul Clappin'.

Billy: — THUH THUH — DAH THUH — THUH THUH —DAH THUH —

Derek got going on the bass.

Deco sang.

— YEH DIDN'T HAVE TO LOVE ME LIKE YEH DID BUT YEH DID BUT YEH DID —

Joey The Lips and Dean: — TRUP —

97

Deco and The Commitmentettes:—AND —
I — THANK — YOU ———
—YEH DIDN'T HAVE TO SQUEEZE ME —
The girls squeezed themselves.
—Get up! someone roared.
— LIKE YEH DID BUT YEH DID BUT
YEH DID —
The horns: — TRUP —
—AND —
I — THANK — YOU ———
A small hand grabbed Bernie's shoe. She stepped
on it and turned.
—AAAH! ——Oh mammy! ——— yeh cunt, yeh.
—Jaysis!
—EVERYDAY —
THERE'S SOMETHIN' NEW ———
YEH PULL OU' YOUR BAG AN' YOUR
BATH IS DUE —
Imelda sniffed under her arm. Someone whis-
tled.
—YEH GOT ME TRYIN' —
NEW THANGS TOO —
JUST —
SO —
I —
CAN KEEP UP WITH YOU ———
YEH DIDN'T HAVE TO SHAKE IT —
The Commitmentettes shook it.
—LIKE YEH DID BUT YEH DID
BUT YEH DID —
The horns: — TRUP —
—AND —
I — THANK — YOU ———

98

YEH DIDN'T HAVE TO MAKE IT —

A mike screeched.

—Sorry 'bou' tha', they heard Jimmy shout. —My fault. ——Won't happen again.

It did though.

So far Outspan hadn't played a chord. He stood looking at the boards, stiff. Deco was prancing up and down (he was used to his suit by now) and Joey The Lips and Dean had been forced back, up against the drums. Natalie's shoes were digging into her. Bernie's hair was coming down.

But they were getting away with it. The thirty-three and Mickah were enjoying the show. They were also expecting Deco to fall off the stage any time now.

So they didn't need Mickah's prompting when I Thank You ended.

—Clap. Go on. ——Clap.

They were clapping already. Mrs Foster was out of her seat. She hadn't noticed that her son hadn't done anything yet.

—Hello, Barrytown, said Deco.

—Hello, Deco!

Deco rubbed his arm across his forehead.

—I hope yis like me group, said Deco.

Those watching the other Commitments saw them stiffening, and Billy making a rude gesture at Deco's back with one of his sticks.

—This one's called Chain Gang.

—HUH ——————

HAH ——————

HUH ——————

HAH ——————

Outspan turned so that he was looking away from his mother. That helped. He began to play, the same chord, but it was a start.

Derek sang.

—WELL DON'T YEH KNOW —

Deco stepped in front of him.

Deco: — THAT'S THE SOUND O' THE MEN —

WORKIN' ON THE CHAIN ——

GA — EE — ANG ——

They were dancing. The audience was dancing, a lot of them, little mods and modettes, shaking, turning in time together, folding their arms, turning, folding their arms, turning. Mickah tried to stop them.

—Just listen, righ'.

But this was their kind of music. Jimmy saw Outspan's mother dancing with them. Mickah had to leave them alone.

Two heavy metallers were leaning against the wall at the side. Mickah went over to them.

—Get dancin', youse.

They started to head-bang.

—Not like tha'.

Mickah stopped them.

—Like them over there.

Back on-stage, an accident was going to happen. It was James' solo and Deco was killing time, swinging the mike over his head. The mike was rising to his right and swooping to his left. It swooped into the back of Bernie's head. She was sent flying forward and she had to jump off the stage.

The Commitments stopped.

There were disappointed Aahs from the crowd and then clapping, Mickah inspired.

Joey The Lips jumped off the stage. There were cheers. Jimmy was down there too, helping them find the heel that had broken off Bernie's shoe. The search kept her mind off the pain at the back of her head.

On-stage, Deco was being given out to.

—Yeh stupid cunt, yeh.

Imelda kicked out at him, and connected. Billy threw a stick at him. It hit his shoulder.

—Yeh were told not to do tha', said Derek.

—I forgot.

—Another thing, said Billy. —It's not YOUR fuckin' group.

—Okay okay, said Deco.

He stood at the edge of the stage. Outspan was looking mean.

—I'm sorry, I'm sorry, righ'.

Bernie came back. She left her shoes and heel in Jimmy's hands. Imelda and Natalie took their shoes off.

—Good girls, Sisters, said Joey The Lips.

He stopped on his way past Deco.

—You apologize very, very nicely to Bernadette or you get my trumpet up your ass.

Deco couldn't believe this. This little baldy fuck was threatening him.

—Move! Joey The Lips roared.

Deco hopped to it.

—Listen, Bernie. ——Sorry, righ'. ——Really.

—Yeah. ——Well, said Bernie.

—Wha' Bernie's tryin' to say, said Imelda, —is tha' you're a stupid bollix.

101

Mickah was singing from behind the crowd.
—WHY ARE WE—

WAI—

TIN'——

—Okay, said Deco into the mike. —Thanks a lot.
Tha' one was dedicated to the lads in jail. Mountjoy
an' tha', who're in for drugs ——like ——because it
must be like a chain gang for them. ——We hope
they get better an'——because, like the banner says,
Heroin Kills.

—So do you.

—Who said tha'? ——Come here, you.

They watched Mickah picking up a child and
carrying him to the door.

—It's not spelt righ', a boy took advantage of
Mickah's absence.

—Fuck off, Smartarse, said Deco. —An'annyway,
if you're ever tryin' to give up the drugs yeh can
always reach ou'.

Nothing happened.

—Billy.

—Wha'?

—Reach Ou'.

—Oh yeah!

—THU — CUDADUNG CUDADUNG
CUDADUNG

—THU — CUDADUNG CUDADUNG
CUDADUNG

Outspan was happier now. Derek had his eyes
closed. Dean wiped his face with his hankie. A drum
fell over. Billy kept going.

——JUST LOOK OVER YOUR SHOUL-
DER, Deco yelled.

102

The Commitmentettes looked over their shoulders.

—THU — CUDADUNG CUDADUNG
CUDADUNG

—THU — CUDADUNG CUDADUNG
CUDADUNG —

—I'LL ——

BE THERE ——

TO LOVE AN' CHERISH —

YOU —

HOU —

OU —

I'LL ——

BE THERE ——

WITH A LOVE THA' IS SO —

TRUE —

HUE —

UE ——

Derek jumped as he thumped at the string and he walked backwards into the piano. James found his fingers on the wrong keys. The piano had moved, bashed into the backdrop, the operetta society's South Pacific scenery (last year's Sound of Music scenery with a very yellow palm tree painted onto one of the hills).

The song was over. The audience didn't know this until Mickah told them to clap.

The caretaker assessed the damage.

—No harm done. ——It's a crummy bloody thing annyway. A spa could paint better than tha', he told Jimmy as the two of them got off the stage.

—How yis doin' ou' there? Deco asked his audience.

—Very well, thanks, said Mrs Foster.

—Okay, said Deco. —This one's for the lads in CIE.

—What's he on abou'? Billy asked James.

He was putting the drum back.

—I just do not know, said James.

—ALL ABOARD, said Deco. —THE NIGHT TRAIN.

The little mods and modettes knew this one. They cheered. They formed a train as The Commitments got going. Joey The Lips and Dean pointed their horns at the lighting. Derek and Outspan shuffled in time together. Deco chugged up and down the front of the stage. The girls went off-stage to have a look at Bernie's shoe. Billy lobbed a stick into the crowd.

No one caught it because everyone was part of the train, Mickah the caboose, going round and round the centre of the hall.

—OH YEAH, Deco started.

OH YEAH——

He swung his arms.

—MIAMI FLORIDA——

ATLANTA GEORGIA——

RALEIGH NORTH CAROLINA——

WASHIN'TON D.C.——

He went off the tracks for a second.

—SOMEWHERE THE FUCK IN WEST VIRGINIA——

BALTIMORE MARYLAND——

PHILADELPH — EYE — AY——

NEW YORK CITY——

HEADIN' HOME——

BOSTON MASSACHU — MASSATUST — YEH KNOW YOURSELF——

104

AN' DON'T FORGET NEW ORLEANS THE
HOME O' THE BLUES ——

OH YEAH ——

THE NIGH' TRAIN ——

THE NIGH' TRAIN ——

COME ON NOW ——

THE NIGH' TRAIN ——

THE NIGH' TRAIN ——

NIGH' TRAIN ——

CARRIES ME HOME —

NIGH' TRAIN ——

CARRIES ME HOME ——

Deco let the other Commitments go on without
him. The important part was coming.

Dublin Soul was about to be born.

He wiped his hands on his trousers. Joey The Lips
gave him the thumbs-up. The Commitmentettes came
back on-stage.

Joey The Lips and Dean were bringing the train
back round towards Deco.

Deco growled: — STARTIN' OFF IN
CONNOLLY ——

The train in the hall stopped as they waited to hear
what was going to follow that.

Deco was travelling north, by DART.

—MOVIN' ON OU' TO KILLESTER ——

They laughed. This was great. They pushed up to
the stage.

—HARMONSTOWN RAHENY ——

They cheered.

—AN' DON'T FORGET KILBARRACK —
THE HOME O' THE BLUES —

Dublin Soul had been delivered.

—HOWTH JUNCTION BAYSIDE ——

THEN ON OU' TO SUTTON WHERE THE
RICH FOLKS LIVE ———
    OH YEAH ———
    NIGH' TRAIN ———
His voice went but he got it back.
—EASY TO BONK YOUR FARE ———
Wild, happy cheers.
—NIGH' TRAIN ———
    AN ALSATIAN IN EVERY CARRI-
AGE ———
    NIGH' TRAIN ———
    LOADS O' SECURITY GUARDS ———
    NIGH' TRAIN ———
    LAYIN' INTO YOUR MOT AT THE
BACK ———
    NIGH' TRAIN ———
    GETTIN' SLAGGED BY YOUR
MATES ———
    NIGH' TRAIN ———
    GETTIN' CHIPS FROM THE CHINESE
CHIPPER ———
    OH NIGH' TRAIN ———
    CARRIES ME HOME —
    THE NIGH' TRAIN ———
    CARRIES ME HOME ———
Two boys invaded the stage and jumped up and
down and went to jump off again. Deco grabbed one
of them and stuck the mike under his mouth.
    —Sing.
    —No way.
    —Go on. NIGH' TRAIN —
The little mod squealed: NIGH' TRAIN.
More of them climbed up on the stage and became

a little choir around the mike-stand.

—NIGH' TRAIN, they roared.

—NIGH' TRAIN, they roared.

—NIGH' TRAIN.

It eventually stopped. The cheering went on for minutes. Derek let himself cry.

Jimmy called them off.

From the side Jimmy spoke into the mike.

—Ladies an' gentlemen, let's hear it for ——Yes, Yes, Yes, The Commitments. ——The Commitments, ladies an' gentlemen. ——The Hardest Workin' Band in the World. ———The Commitments —— bringing soul to Dublin —— Bringing the People's Music to the People. ——Yes, Yes, Yes, Yes —The Commitments.

Mickah dug his finger into backs.

—Shout for more. Go on. ——More.

—MORE!

—More!

—We can't hear yis, said Jimmy.

—Where d'yeh think you're goin'? said Mickah.

—Home, said a boy.

—Get back up there an' cheer. ——Go on.

—I have to go home. ——Me ma will burst me.

—I'll burst yeh if yeh don't get back.

—We can't hear yis, said Jimmy.

He put his hand over the mike.

—What Becomes of the Broken Hearted, then the girls do Stoned Love, then yis come off again, then Knock on Wood, righ'? ——Got tha'?

—Wha' abou' Man's World?

—They're too young, said Jimmy.

—When a Man Loves a Woman?

107

—Too slow, said Jimmy. —They'd get bored. They're too young. A couple o' fast ones is enough for them.

—But we rehearsed loads more, said Derek.

—Brother Jimmy speaks the truth, said Joey The Lips. —A short, sharp shock works best with the very young Brothers and Sisters.

The caretaker arrived.

—There's a fella at the back, from tha' Northside News thing.

—Fame, said James. —I'm gonna live till Tuesday.

—Janey! said Natalie. —Does he have a camera?

—Yeah, he does, said the caretaker. —He's a bag full o' them. Flashes an' ———— yeh know.

Jimmy spoke into the mike.

—They're comin' back, ladies an' gentlemen, The Commitments are comin' back.

He pointed to James.

—Clap hands clap hands for James The Soul Surgeon Clifford.

Deco pushed James onto the stage. James stood there.

—The man performs transplants on the piano, ladies an' gentlemen. ———Soul Surgeon Clifford.

James went over to the piano.

—On drums, Billy The Animal Mooney.

Billy jumped on-stage and gorilla-walked to his drums.

One at a time Jimmy sent them back. Joey The Lips got the biggest cheer.

The girls were last.

—Last, said Jimmy. —The girls.

There were screams. The girls looked at one another and raised their eyes to heaven.

—Sonya ——Sofia ——An' Tanya. ——The Commitmentettes, ladies an' gentlemen.

They strolled onto the stage. Natalie ducked when she saw something fly up and out of the darkness. It landed behind them, a little pair of light blue underpants.

The Commitments cracked up. Deco kicked the underpants off the stage. They came back. Deco kicked them across to Jimmy.

—Okay, y'awl, said Deco to the fans. —Let's take it to the bridge.

—I'll get them back for yeh after, righ', said Mickah. —When it's over.

—Yeh said yeh'd give me a pound, the boy reminded him.

—I'll let yeh in for nothin' the next time, said Mickah.

This injustice stunned the boy for a while. He'd just made a sap of himself, flinging his kaks at your women on the stage and now he wasn't even going to be paid for it. Then words came back to him.

—Yeh fuckin' bollix, yeh.

Mickah gave him a good dig, then felt guilty and gave the boy fifty pence, and another dig.

Most of the encore went well. The little mods recognized What Becomes of the Broken Hearted and they cheered when Deco sang the bit about waiting under Clery's clock.

—Thank you, little Brothers and Sisters, said Joey The Lips. —The Lord Jesus smiles down on you. Thank you. ——Now the Sisters, Sonya, Sofia and

109

Tanya, are going to cut loose. ——Brothers and
Sisters, The Commitmentettes.

—Whooo! said Deco. —Let's take it to the bridge.

—Wha' fuckin' bridge?

—Who said tha'? Mickah roared.

—Matt Talbot bridge.

—Who said tha'?

Deco wouldn't get out of the girls' way. He stood
his ground at the front, leering at his audience.

Billy shouted: —Get ou' o' the fuckin' way.

—Stay cool, said Deco.

He handed the mike to Imelda. She stung his ear
with it.

And they were off. Against The Commitments' best
ever, tightest thumping back-beat, the girls bleated
Stoned Love. They swayed, clapped their hands,
stopped. And before the crowd could start screaming,
they started again. Jimmy had to climb up onto the
stage to gently shove the small boys and girls back
off.

Deco came back on and Knock on Wood began. It
ended early when he knocked over the horn section's
mike and half the horn section gave him an almighty
kick up the hole.

Deco wasn't going to be able to sing again for a
good few minutes so Jimmy drew the curtain. James
and Billy looked at Deco kneeling on the floor, bent
forward.

—Tha' took him to the bridge, said Billy.

—Quite, said James.

—He was lookin' for it, Dean was explaining to
Jimmy.

—Could yeh not have waited till he stopped singin'?

110

said Jimmy. —Or at least till he got to the end o' the sentence.

Outspan laughed.

The first gig was over.

Mickah's head appeared from under the curtain.

—Hey, Jimmy, he said. —There's a sap here from ——Hang on.

Mickah was gone. And back.

—The Northside News. ——He wants a word.

When Jimmy drew the curtain back they all saw the sap from Northside News. He was tall, young, with tinted glasses.

—Great gig, said the sap from the Northside News. —Who's in charge?

—I'm the singer, Deco told him.

—For the time being, said Jimmy.

—Well said, Jimmy, said Outspan.

—Pack the gear, lads, said Jimmy. —Keep the suits on but. ——For the snaps. ——Joey, come on.

Jimmy jumped off the stage. He shook the sap's hand.

They introduced themselves.

—An' this is Joey The Lips Fagan, said Jimmy.

—Hi.

—Good evening, Brother.

—Will we be in next Friday's one? Mickah asked the sap.

—Give Billy a hand with his kit, will yeh, Mickah.

Mickah grabbed Jimmy's fringe.

—Say please.

—Please, Mickah.

Mickah grinned.

—Certainly. ——No problem.

111

—Our security man, Jimmy explained.

—The price of fame, said Joey The Lips.

—Right, said the sap.

He had a notebook.

—When were you formed?

—Some months back, said Joey The Lips.

—How did the band come about?

Jimmy spoke. —Well, I put an ——

—Destiny, said Joey The Lips. —It was destined to happen.

Jimmy liked the sound of that so he let Joey The Lips keep talking.

—My man, said Joey The Lips. —We are a band with a mission.

—A mission?

—You hear good and you hear right.

The sap looked to Jimmy but Jimmy said nothing.

—What kind of mission d'you mean?

—An important mission, Brother.

Jimmy leaned over to Joey The Lips and whispered:
—Don't mention God.

Joey The Lips smiled.

—We are bringing Soul to Dublin, Brother, he said.
—We are bringing the music, the Soul, back to the people. ——The proletariat. ——That's p,r,o,l,e,-t,a,r,i,a,t.

—Thanks a lot.

Jimmy spoke. —We're against racial and sexual discrimination an' heroin, isn't tha' righ', Joey?

—That is right, said Joey The Lips.

—We ain't gonna play Sun City, said Jimmy.

—Tell the people, Joey The Lips told the sap, —to put on their soul shoes because The Com-

mitments are coming and there's going to be dancing in the streets.

—This'll make good copy, said the sap.

—And there'll be barricades in the streets too, said
Joey The Lips. —Now you've got great copy.

—Wow, said the sap. —Nice one. ——When's
your next gig?

—My friend, said Joey The Lips. —We are the
Guerrillas of Soul. We do not announce our gigs. We
hit, and then we sink back into the night.

Jimmy tapped the sap's shoulder.

—I think there's a U in Guerrillas.

—Oh yeah. ——Thanks a lot.

—Do yeh want to take a few photographs?

—Yeah, right.

—Joey, make sure their ties are all on straigh', will
yeh?

—I obey.

Joey The Lips sat on a chair. The Commitments
kneeled and stood around him. Bernie sat on his knee.
Imelda lay in front of him, leaning on an elbow, chin
in her hand, hair in her eyes. Natalie did the same, in
the opposite direction. Jimmy, Mickah, the caretaker
and Mrs Foster stood at the sides, like football managers
and magic-sponge men. That way they all fitted.

* * *

There was nothing for a few weeks.

The Commitments rehearsed.

Jimmy did the round of the music pubs in town.
One of them only did heavy metal groups. The
manager explained to Jimmy that the heavy metal

113

crowd was older and very well behaved, and drank like fish.

A barman in another one told Jimmy that the manager only booked groups that modelled themselves on Echo and The Bunnymen because they were always reviewed and the reviews usually included praise for the manager and his pioneering work.

On the fourth night Jimmy found a pub that would take The Commitments for one night, a Thursday, no fee, but three free pints each. The head barman was a big Motown fan and he and the Northside News headline (Soul Soldiers of Destiny) convinced the owner.

Jimmy couldn't figure out how it got the name The Regency Rooms. There was only one room, about ten times bigger than his bedroom. The walls were stained and bare. The floor was stained and bare. The stools and chairs showed their guts. The stage was a foot-high plywood platform.

—They won't all fit, said Mickah.

—I know tha', said Jimmy. —Billy will, an' the girls an' Outspan an' Derek. Put the piano over there at the jacks door, righ', an' Joey an' Dean can go over there an' Deco in the middle. An' the mixer on the table there.

—Good thinkin'.

When the head barman came in to work he went for Jimmy.

—You didn't tell us it was a fuckin' orchestra we were bookin', he screamed.

—I thought yeh'd know, said Jimmy. —Yeh said yeh were a Motown fan.

—The wife has The Supremes' Greatest Hits. ———
It's the same size as any other record.

—We've squashed them all in, said Jimmy.

—Yeah. ———An' yis still take up half the fuckin'
pub. ———Look. The piano. ———Yeh'd usually get
abou' twenty into tha' corner.

—Yeh would in your bollix, said Mickah. ——
Fuckin' leprechauns maybe. ———Or test-tube babies.

—Mickah.

—Wha'?

—The drums.

—Okay.

—Anyway, said the head barman when Mickah was
a safe distance away, —this is the last time yis'll be
playin' here. Nothin' personal now but we can't afford
the space. We usually do groups with just three in
them.

He thought of something else.

—Another thing. ———There's no way we're givin'
yis three pints each. We couldn't. ———One'll have to do.

—Ah, fuck tha'! said Jimmy.

—There's millions of yis, said the head barman.
———You can have the three though. Just make it
look like you're payin' me.

Jimmy looked around him.

—Okay. ———Done.

There was a good crowd. Thirty would have been
a great crowd in this place. The room was packed solid.
The ones standing up had to hold their glasses up above
their shoulders.

—An older bunch this time, Jimmy pointed out. ——
This'll be a better concert ——— gig. More adult ori-
entated. Know wha' I mean?

The Commitments stood around the platform waiting for the go ahead from the head barman.

—These people have votes, said Jimmy. —This is our real audience.

Outspan stood on the platform searching the crowd for his mother. He didn't think she'd have the neck to come to this one but he wanted to make sure.

Jimmy picked his way over to Mickah.

—Listen, he said. —They have their own bouncer here so ——just enjoy the show, righ'.

—I was talkin' to him, Mickah told him. —He's goin' to give me a shout if there's anny messin'.

—That'll be nice, said Jimmy.

He got behind his desk. A mike screeched.

It was half-nine. The head barman gave Jimmy the nod. Jimmy got up and took Deco's mike.

—Ladies an' gentlemen, The Regency Rooms presents, all the way from Dublin, (that didn't get the laughs he'd been expecting). The Hardest Workin' Band in the World, The Saviours of Soul ——Yes, Yes, Yes, Yes ———The Commitments.

They were sharper this time. Billy knew what he was doing. Outspan didn't have his ma gawking up at him. Deco was hemmed in by tables on three sides and by Dean and Joey The Lips behind him. He couldn't budge. There'd be no accidents tonight.

Natalie fell off the platform. But it wasn't an accident. Imelda pushed her. They were only messing.

The songs were going down well. They were sticking to the classics, the ones everyone knew. The Dublined lyrics were welcomed with laughter and, towards closing time, cheers and clapping. The Commitmentettes were whistled at, but politely.

116

One man roared: —Get them off yeh!

Mickah advised him to stay quiet.

Deco's between-songs chat was better. Jimmy and Joey The Lips had been coaching him.

He was still a prick though, Jimmy had to admit to Mickah.

Night Train was a very big hit. There wasn't room for an audience train but the ones standing rocked up and down and the ones sitting stood.

It was over. The Commitments couldn't leave the stage, unless they all piled into the jacks, so they stayed at the platform while the audience clapped and cheered, and waited for Jimmy to take over.

—More!

—Yes, Yes, Yes, ladies an' gentlemen —— comrades. You've heard the people's music tonight. ——The Commitments, ladies an' gentlemen. —— The Saviours o' Soul. ——Do yis want to hear more?

They wanted more.

Jimmy handed Deco the mike.

—Introduce the lads.

—Okay, said Deco into the mike. —I'd better introduce the rest. ——On drums, Billy Mooney. ——On guitar ——If yeh could hear it, ha ha ——Outspan sorry, L. Terence Foster. Derek, there on bass. —— James Soul Surgeon Clifford is the specky guy on the joanna.

Each Commitment was being clapped but The Commitments weren't hearing it. All Commitment eyes were burning Deco. This wasn't what they'd rehearsed, at all.

—Dean Fay on the sax there, righ', an' Joey The

Lips Fagan on the trumpet. Joey on the horn, wha'.
——An' they're Tanya, Sonya an' Sofia, The
Commitmentettes. I'm Deco Blanketman Cuffe and
we are The Commitments. This one's called When a
Man Loves a Woman.

Deco climbed up on a vacant stool.

—THU —CUDADUNG CUDADUNG
CUDADUNG —

Billy blammed out the Reach Out — I'll Be There
beat, then stopped. He got out from behind the drums
and went across to the jacks.

James played, then Derek, then Deco started to
sing.

—WHEN A MA — HAN LOVES A WO —
MAN ——

CAN'T KEEP HIS MIND ON NOTHIN '
EH — ELSE ——

HE'LL CHANGE THE WORLD —

FOR THE GOOD THINGS HE'S FOU —
HOUND ——

IF SHE'S BA — HAD HE CAN'T SEE —
IT ——

SHE CAN DO NO WRO — O — ON — NG

TURN HIS BACK ON HIS BEST FRIEND IF
HE PUT HER DOWN ——

It was beautiful. Jimmy blinked. The Commitments
were forgiving Deco. Billy was still in the jacks
though. The head barman sent a fourth pint over to
Jimmy, and even one for Mickah.

—WHEN THIS —
MAN LOVES THIS WO —
MAN ——

118

Outspan's rhythm playing was just right here, light and jangly.

—AN' GIVES HER EVERYTHING ON EARTH ————

Outspan swayed.

—TRYIN' TO HOLD ONTO ————

   YOUR —

   CROCK O' GOLD ————

   BABY —

   PLEASE DON'T —

   TREAT ME BA — AA — AA — AAD ————
————

The crowd oohed.

—WHEN A MA — HAN LOVES A WO —
                      MAN ————

   HE'LL BUY HER LOADS O' SWE — EE
—EETS ————

   HE'LL EVEN BRING HER TO STUPID PLACES LIKE THE ZOO — OO ————

   HE'LL SPEND ALL HIS WAGES ON —
                      HER ————

   BUT DON'T LET HIM SEE YEH LOOKIN' AT HER ————

   COS HE'LL GET A HAMMER AN' HE'LL FUCKIN' CREASE YOU ————

No one laughed. It wasn't funny. It was true.

—YES WHEN A MA — HAN LOVES A
                  WO — MAN —

   I KNOW EXACTLY HOW HE FEEL — YELLS —

   COS —

   BABY —

   BABY —

119

BABY

I LOVE YOU ———

It was over. The lights went off and on and off and on. Friends came up to congratulate The Commitments.

—You've a great voice, a woman told Deco.

—I don't need you to tell me tha', said Deco.

Billy came out of the jacks. Before he could be asked if he was alright, he'd made it over to his drums and picked up a stick. He stepped over to Deco and started to hit him on the neck and shoulders with it.

He chanted as he walloped.

—I'm Billy—— The Animal Mooney, d'yeh ———hear me? Billy The —— Animal Mooney an' we all ———have stage names an' you know fuckin' ————well wha' they are, yeh lousy ——bollix yeh, we're not your group, we're ———not your fuckin' ——group ——

Mickah held his arms down. Deco got out from under him.

—Yeh were lookin' for tha', said Jimmy.

—Wha' did I do now? Deco asked.

—Oh look it! said Bernie. —He's after burstin' one of his plukes.

Most of The Commitments laughed.

—Yeh didn't introduce the group properly, said Jimmy.

I forgot.

—Fuck off!

—I was oney jokin'. Yis have no sense o' humour, d'yis know tha'?

—An' you have? Outspan asked.

—Yeah.

120

—You've a big head too, pal.

—You're just jealous ——

—Fuck off.

—All o' yis.

—Enough, said Joey The Lips.

—Jealous o' you? ——Huh ——

—Enough.

—Joey's righ', said Jimmy. —We'll meet tomorrow nigh' an' have this ou'.

Deco left.

—Watch ou' for the fans, Derek shouted after him.

Mickah let go of Billy.

—He's ruinin' everythin', Jimmy, said Billy. —I'm sorry abou' tha', yeh know. But I'm sick of him. It was great an' then he ——— He's a fuckin' cunt.

—That's an accurate description, said James.

—I'll kill him the next time, said Billy. —I will. —— I will now.

—He's not worth it, said Derek.

—He is, Billy, said Imelda. —Kill him.

—Ah, for fuck sake! said Jimmy.

—I'm oney messin', said Imelda. —Don't kill him, Billy.

—Yeah, said Natalie. —Just give him a hidin'.

—I'll do tha' for yis if yeh want, said Mickah.

—Brothers, said Joey The Lips.

His palms were lifted. The Commitments were ready to listen to him.

—Now, Brother Deco might not be the most likeable of the Brothers ——

—He's a prick, Joey.

—He is, Brother Dean. I admit I agree. Brother Deco is a prick. He is a prick. But the voice, Brothers

121

and Sisters. ——His voice is not the voice of a prick. That voice belongs to God.

No one argued with him.

—We need him, Brothers. We need the voice.

—Pity abou' the rest of him.

—Granted.

—I'll talk to him tomorrow at work, said Jimmy.

—Tell him I'll kill him.

* * *

The Commitments got a mention in the Herald.

—The Commitments, said the mention, —played a strong Motown(ish) set. New to the live scene, they were at times ragged but always energetic. Their suits didn't fit them properly. My companion fell in love with the vocalist, a star surely in the ascendant. I hate him! (—Oh fuck! said Jimmy.) Warts and all, The Commitments are a good time. They might also be important. See them.

* * *

Armed with this and the Northside News article, Jimmy got The Commitments a Wednesday night in another pub, a bigger one, The Miami Vice (until recently The Dark Rosaleen). It was a bit on the southside, but near the DART.

The Commitments went down well again. Deco stuck to the rehearsed lines. Everyone went home happy.

They were given a month's residency, Wednesdays. They could charge two pounds admission if they could fill the pub the first night.

122

They filled it.

A certain type of audience was coming to see them. The crowds reminded Jimmy of the ones he'd been part of at the old Blades gigs. They were older and wiser now, grown-up mods. Their clothes were more adventurous but they were still neat and tidy. The women's hairstyles were more varied. They weren't really modettes any more.

A good audience, Jimmy decided. The mods and ex-mods knew good music when they heard it. Their dress was strict but they listened to anything good, only, mind you, if the musicians dressed neatly.

The Commitments were neat. Jimmy was happy with the audience. So was Joey The Lips. These were The People.

Another thing Jimmy noticed: they were shouting for Night Train.

—NIGH' TRAIN, Deco screeched.

OH SWEE' MOTHER O' JAYSIS —

NIGH' TRAIN —

OH SWEE' MOTHER O' FUCKIN' JAYSIS —

NIGH' TRAIN —

NIGH' TRAIN —

NIGH' TRAIN ——

COME ON ——

The Commitmentettes lifted their right arms and pulled the whistle cords.

—WHHWOO WOOO —

—NIGH'

Deco wiped his forehead and opened his neck buttons.

—TRAIN.

—More!

—MORE!

123

They shouted for more, but that was it. Three times in one night was enough.

—Thank y'awl, said Deco. —We're The Commitments. ——Good nigh' an' God bless.

—We should make a few shillin's next week an' annyway, wha', said Mickah.

He was collecting the mikes.

—Brother Jimmy, said Joey The Lips. —I'm worried. ——About Dean.

—Wha' abou' Dean?

—He told me he's been listening to jazz.

—What's wrong with tha'? Jimmy wanted to know.

—Everything, said Joey The Lips. —Jazz is the antithesis of soul.

—I beg your fuckin' pardon!

—I'll go along with Joey there, said Mickah.

—See, said Joey The Lips. —Soul is the people's music. Ordinary people making music for ordinary people. ——Simple music. Any Brother can play it. The Motown sound, it's simple. Thump-thump-thump-thump. ——That's straight time. Thump-thump-thump-thump. ——See? Soul is democratic, Jimmy. Anyone with a bin lid can play it. ——It's the people's music.

—Yeh don't need anny honours in your Inter to play soul, isn't tha' wha' you're gettin' at, Joey?

—That's right, Brother Michael.

—Mickah.

—Brother Mickah. That's right. You don't need a doctorate to be a doctor of soul.

—Nice one.

—An' what's wrong with jazz? Jimmy asked.

—Intellectual music, said Joey The Lips. —It's anti-people music. It's abstract.

—It's cold an' emotionless, amn't I righ'? said Mickah.

—You are. ——It's got no soul. It is sound for the sake of sound. It has no meaning. ——It's musical wanking, Brother.

—Musical wankin', said Mickah. —That's good. ——Here, yeh could play tha' at the Christmas parties. ——Instead o' musical chairs.

—What's Dean been listenin' to? Jimmy asked.

—Charlie Parker.

—He's supposed to be good but.

—Good! Joey The Lips gasped. —The man had no right to his black skin.

Joey The Lips was getting worked up. It was some sight. They stood back and enjoyed it.

—They should have burnt it off with a fucking blow lamp.

—Language, Joey!

—Polyrhythms! Polyrhythms! I ask you! That's not the people's sound. ——Those polyrhythms went through Brother Parker's legs and up his ass. —— And who did he play to? I'll tell you, middle-class white kids with little beards and berets. In jazz clubs. Jazz clubs! They didn't even clap. They clicked their fingers.

Joey The Lips clicked his fingers.

—Like that. ——I'll tell you something, Brothers. ——I've never told anyone this before.

They waited.

—The biggest regret of my life is that I wasn't born black.

—Is tha' righ', Joey?

—Charlie Parker was born black. A beautiful, shiny, bluey sort of black. ——And he could play. He could play alright. But he abused it, he spat on it. He turned his back on his people so he could entertain hip honky brats and intellectuals. ——Jazz! It's decadent. —— The Russians were right. They banned it.

Joey The Lips was calmer now. He stopped picking at his sleeve.

—The Bird! he spat. ——And that's what poor Dean is listening to.

—Sounds bad alrigh'.

—Oh, it's bad. ——Very bad. Parker, John Coltrane —— Herbie Hancock ——— and the biggest motherfucker of them all, Miles Davis.

———Em, why does it worry you, exactly?

—We're going to lose him.

—Wha' d'yeh mean?

—Dean is going to become a Jazz Purist.

The words almost made Joey The Lips retch.

—He won't want to play for the people any more. Dean has soul but he's going to kill it if he listens to jazz. Jazz is for the mind.

—Wha' can we do? said Jimmy.

—We can give him a few digs, said Mickah.

—Mickah.

—Wha'?

—The drums.

—Okay.

* * *

Hot Press came to the second gig of the resi-

126

dency, and paid in because Mickah wouldn't believe him.

—I'm from the Hot Press.

—I'm from the kitchen press, said Mickah. —It's two quid or fuck off.

Mickah took in one hundred and twenty pounds. It made a great bulge in his shirt pocket. He showed it to James.

—The big time, wha'.

Jimmy studied Dean for tell-tale signs. There weren't many, but they were there. Dean hunched over the sax now, protecting it. He used to throw it up and out and pull himself back, to let everyone see its shininess. It wouldn't be long before he'd be sitting on a stool when he was playing. The stool definitely wasn't soul furniture. Jimmy was upset. He liked Dean.

Deco was his usual self. It was a pity his voice was so good. Jimmy didn't pay much attention to Billy.

This was a pity. Because Billy left The Commitments, just before the encore.

—On yeh go, Bill, said Jimmy.

—I can't, said Billy.

—Why not?

—I've left.

A long gap, then —Wha'?

—I've left. I'm not goin' back on. ——I've left.

—Jaysis! said Jimmy.

When a Man Loves a Woman didn't need drums.

—James, Jimmy roared. —Fire away.

—Now, said Jimmy. —Tell your Uncle Jimmy all abou' it.

—I just ——

Jimmy could see Billy thinking.

—It's just ——I hate him, Jimmy. I fuckin' hate him ——I can't even sleep at nigh'.

Billy's face was clenched.

—Why's tha'?

—I stay awake tryin' to think o' better ways to hate him. ——Imaginin', yeh know, ways to kill him.

Billy looked straight at Jimmy.

—I phoned his house yesterday. Can yeh believe tha'? I never done ann'thin' like tha' before. No way. ——His oul' one —I s'pose it was his oul' one annyway ——answered. I said nothin'. ——I just listened.

—Yeh'd want to get a grip on yourself, son. You're talkin' like a fuckin' spacer.

—I know, I fuckin' know. Do yeh not think I know? ——That's why I've left. I never want to have to look at the cunt again. ——Want to get him ou' o' me life, know wha' I mean? ——I made up me mind durin' I Thank You. The way he was shovin' his arse into your women at the front. It was fuckin' disgustin'. ——Annyway I've left, so ——I've left.

—He's not worth hatin'.

—He fuckin' is, yeh know.

Jimmy looked at Billy. He'd left alright. There was no point trying to talk him back in. That made Jimmy angry.

—Annyone can play the drums, Billy. ——So fuck off.

—Ah, Jimmy!

—Go an' shite.

—I want me drums.

128

—After the gig.

—It's my van, remember.

—We'll hire a van. No, we'll buy one. A better one than your scabby van.

Jimmy was going over to the platform but he turned back to Billy.

—A light blue one with The Commitments written on the side in dark blue. An' Billy The Animal Mooney Is A Bollox on the back, righ'.

Billy said nothing.

When a Man Loves a Woman was over. They were going to do Knock on Wood now.

Jimmy got a drum stick and stood behind a snare drum.

The others watched.

—Righ', said Jimmy. —Are yis righ'?

—BLAM —

—Come on.

—BLAM —

—James, come on.

—BLAM —

By the end of Knock on Wood Jimmy thought he'd proved his point: anyone could play the drums.

It had been a great gig, Hot Press told Jimmy. Dublin needed something like The Commitments, to get U2 out of its system. He'd be doing a review for the next issue. Then he asked for his two pounds back.

* * *

The Commitments didn't see Billy again. He didn't live in Barrytown.

129

Mickah called for Jimmy on Friday. There was a rehearsal in Joey The Lips' mother's garage. When they got to the bus stop Mickah spoke.

—Jimmy, have I ever asked yeh for annythin'?

—Yeah.

Mickah hadn't banked on that answer.

—When?

—Yeh asked me for a lend o' me red biro in school. To rule a margin because E.T. said as far as he was concerned your homework wasn't done till it had a margin.

—Jimmy, said Mickah. —I'm bein' serious. Now will yeh treat me with a little respect, okay. Now have I ever asked yeh for annythin'?

—No.

—That's better. ——Well, I'm goin' to ask yeh for somethin' now.

—I've no money.

—Jimmy, said Mickah. —I'm tryin' me best. But I'm goin' to have to hit yeh.

He was leaning into Jimmy.

—Wha' is it? said Jimmy.

—Let me play the drums.

—I was goin' ——

—Let me play the drums.

—Fair enough.

* * *

So Mickah was the new drummer. He even had a name for himself.

—Eh, Washin'ton D.C. Wallace.

The Commitments laughed. It was good.

130

—The D.C. stands for Dead Cool, said Mickah.

—Oh yeah, said Imelda. —That's very clever, tha' is.

They were waiting for Dean and James.

Joey The Lips spoke. —We have lost The Animal, Brothers and Sisters. We'll miss him. But we have a good man in his place, a city of a man. Washington D.C.

Jimmy took over.

—We've had our first crisis, righ', but we're over it. We're still The Commitments. An' we're reachin' our audience. Yeh saw tha' yourselves on Wednesday.

Jimmy let them remember Wednesday for a bit. It had been a good night.

—We'll dedicate our first album to Billy.

—We will in our holes, said Outspan.

—Ahh ——why not? said Bernie.

—We'd have to pay him.

—Would we?

—Fuck him so.

Joey The Lips went into the house to answer the phone.

Dean arrived while Joey The Lips was gone. He'd had his hair cropped.

—Jaysis, Dean, wha'.

He was wearing his shades.

—Dean, your shirt's gorgeous.

—Thanks.

Joey The Lips came back.

—Brother James on the telephone, Brothers. He can't make it. He has a mother of an examination. ———Tomorrow.

Joey The Lips had just seen Dean.

131

—Is the wattage of the bulb too strong for you, Dean?

Outspan and Derek laughed.

—It's the flowers on his shirt he's protectin' his eyes from, said Deco.

—Leave him alone. It's lovely.

Jimmy clapped his hands.

—Let's get goin'. ——Come on. We'll keep it short.

—Yeah, said Bernie. —Rehearsals are borin'.

—We need some fresh tunes, said Joey The Lips.

He patted Bernie's shoulder.

—Let's break Mickah in first, said Jimmy.

—That's Washin'ton D.C. durin' office hours, said Mickah.

He was behind the drum. There was only the one.

—Can we call yeh Washah for short? said Outspan.

—Yeh can, said Mickah, —but you'll get a hidin' for yourself.

—Washin'ton D.C., said Derek. —That's a deadly name, Mickah.

Mickah smacked the drum.

—Nothin' to it.

He smacked it again.

—That's fuckin' grand. ——Child's play.

—Try it with both sticks.

He did.

—There. ——How was tha'?

—Grand.

—Can we go home now? said Mickah.

Mickah was a good addition. The Commitments liked him and his enthusiasm came at the right time. They enjoyed his mistakes and his questions. They

132

rehearsed again on Monday night. They wanted Mickah ready for Wednesday.

Mickah took the drum home with him. His da, the only harder man than Mickah in Barrytown, burned the sticks. His ma bought him a new set.

*　*　*

The Commitments were a revitalized outfit on the third Wednesday of the residency. They all arrived on time. The Commitmentettes had new tights, with little black butterflies behind the ankles. Mickah wore Jimmy's suit. James had a bottle of Mister Sheen. He polished the piano.

—More elbow grease there, said Outspan.

Jimmy took in the money at the door, one hundred and forty-six pounds. That meant thirteen more people than the week before. And that didn't include Hot Press and the three others with him he'd let in for nothing.

The Commitments played well.

Outspan and Derek had become very confident. The Commitmentettes were brilliant. They looked great, very glossy, and their sense of humour showed in their stage movements.

They were enjoying themselves.

Mickah tapped and thumped happily on the drum, sometimes using his fingers or his fist, once his fore-head. His shoulders jumped as he drummed, way up over his ears.

One thing spoiled Jimmy's enjoyment: Dean's solo in Stop in the Name of Love. The Commitmentettes were at their best. They raised their right hands every

133

time they sang STOP. Then they'd spin quickly before they continued with IN THE NAME OF LOVE. Mickah kept his eyes on them and his timing and their timing were perfect.

Dean's solo was good. It was really good, but it was new. It wasn't the one he'd always done.

Joey The Lips explained what was wrong with it later.

—Soul solos have corners. They fit into the thump-thump-thump-thump. The solo is part of the song. Are you with me?

—No.

—Strictly speaking, Brother, soul solos aren't really solos at all.

—Ah, Jaysis, Joey ——

—Shhh ——— There are no gaps in soul. If it doesn't fit it isn't used. Soul is community. As Little Richard says, If It Don't Fit Don't Force It. Do you understand now?

—Sort of.

—Dean's solo didn't have corners. It didn't fit. It spiralled. It wasn't part of the song. ——It wasn't part of anything. It was a real solo. Washington D.C.'s drumming wasn't there as far as it was concerned. ——That's jazz, Brother. That's what jazz does. It makes the man selfish. He doesn't give a fuck about his Brothers. That's what jazz is doing to Dean, said Joey The Lips. —Poor Dean.

The Commitments finished with It's a Man's Man's Man's World. Mickah stood back. James gave the beat out here.

—DOOM — DAH DAH DAH DAH DAH —
DOOM — DAH DAH DAH DAH DAH —

134

Deco sang: —THIS IS A MAN — AN'S WORLD
——

The Commitmentettes shook their heads.
—DOOM — DAH DAH DAH DAH DAH —
DOOM — DAH DAH DAH DAH DAH —
—THIS IS A MA — AN'S WORLD ———
The girls shook their heads again. Some men in the
audience cheered.
—BUT IT WOULDN'T BE NOTHIN' —
NOTHIN' ———
WITHOU' ——
A WOMAN OR A GURL ——
The Commitmentettes nodded. They turned to
look at Deco. He was facing them.
—YEH KNOW ——
MAN MADE THE CAR —
THA' TAKES US ONTO THE RO — OAD
——

MAN MADE THE TRAY — AY — YAIN —
TO CARRY THE HEAVY LOAD ——
—DOOM — DAH DAH DAH DAH DAH —
DOOM ——DAH DAH DAH DAH DAH——
The Commitmentettes turned their backs on Deco.
He pleaded with them.
—MAN MADE THE 'LECTRIC LIGH' ——
The girls looked over their shoulders at him.
—TO TAKE US OU' O' THE DA — HARK
——

MAN MADE THE BOAT FOR THE WAT
—HAH ——
LIKE NOAH MADE THE AH — ARK ———
Outspan plucked the guitar like a harp.
—COS IT'S A MAN'S —

135

MAN'S —
　　　　MAN'S WORLD ——
BUT IT WOULDN'T BE NOTHIN' —
NOTHIN' ——
WITHOU' A WOMAN OR A GURREL ——

The girls swayed and nodded. Mickah swayed and
nodded.

—YEH SEE ——

Deco was still singing to the girls.

—MAN DRIVES THE BUSES ——
　　　TO BRING US ROUN' AN' ABOU — OU'
——

AN' MAN WORKS IN GUINNESSES ——
　　　TO GIVE US THE PINTS O' STOU — OUT
——

The crowd began to clap here. Deco raised his
hands, and the clapping stopped.

—AN' MAN —
MAN HAS ALL THE IMPORTANT JOBS
——

LIKE HE COLLECTS ALL THE TAXES
——

BUT WOMAN —
WOMAN ONLY WORKS UP IN
CADBURY'S ——
PUTTIN' CHOCOLATES INTO BOXES ——
SO —
SO —
SO —
IT'S A MAN'S — MAN'S WORLD —
BUT IT WOULD BE NOTHIN' —
NOTHIN' —
FUCK ALL ——
WITHOU' A WOMAN OR A GURREL ——

136

This time they wouldn't stop cheering and clapping, so It's a Man's Man's Man's World was over.

The Commitments were clearing the stage after closing time.

Derek spoke. —Tha' Man's World is a rapid song, isn't it?

—Fuckin' brilliant.

Deco took the bottle from his mouth.

—Yeah, he said. —I'm thinkin' o' doin' it on Screen Test. ——Tha' or When a Man Loves a Woman. They're me best.

Outspan dropped everything.

—There's no way we're goin' on Screen Test. No fuckin' way.

—Yeah, said Derek.

—I know tha', said Deco. —Yis didn't hear me.

He took a mouthful from the bottle.

—Did I not tell yis? ——I thought I did. ——No, I'm goin' on Screen Test. On me own, like. I got me ma' to write in for me.

Derek roared. —JIMMY! COME EAAR!

Then he stared at Deco.

Jimmy was just outside on the path, thanking Hot Press for coming. He heard the roar.

—Good fuck! I'd better get in. ——Migh' see yeh again next week so?

—Right, yeah.

—An' see if yeh can bring your man along, righ'. I'll buy him a pint.

—Will do.

Jimmy trotted in. He had good news.

He forgot it when he saw the story; The Commitments standing away from one another, Deco in the middle.

137

—Wha' now?

—Tell him, said Derek.

Deco told Jimmy.

—Yeh bad shite, yeh, said Jimmy.

—Wha'!

—Are yeh serious?

—Yeah. ——I am.

—What is this Screen Test? Joey The Lips asked.

Outspan told him.

—It's a poxy programme on RTE. A talent show like.

—It's fuckin' terrible, Joey, said Derek.

—Sounds uncool, said Joey The Lips.

—Why didn't yeh tell us? Jimmy asked Deco.

—I did tell yis.

No one backed him up.

—I remember tellin' some o' yis. ——I told you, James.

—No.

—I must've. ———I meant to.

Mickah came out of the jacks.

—Sorry abou' tha', said Deco. —Yeah ——annyway, the ma wrote in for me.

Deco decided to get all the confessing over with.

—I applied to sing in the National Song Contest as well.

—Oh ——my——Jaysis!

—I don't believe yeh, said Dean.

The Commitmentettes were starting to laugh.

—Well, said Deco. —Let's put it this way. —— I've me career to think of.

Mickah started laughing. Deco didn't know if this was good or bad.

138

James laughed too.

—Have yeh no fuckin' loyalty, son? said Jimmy. —You're in a fuckin' group.

—A Song for Europe! said Outspan. —Fuckin' God! ——Wha'.

Imelda sang: —ALL KINDS —
                            OF EVERYTHIN' —
                            REMINDS ME —
                                              OF —
                                                 YOU.

—Ah, fuck off, said Deco. —Look. ——The group won't last forever.

—Not with you in it.

—Look. ——Be realistic, will yeh. ——I can sing, righ'. ——

—That's not soul, Brother, Joey The Lips told Deco.

—Fuck off, you, said Deco, —an' don't annoy me.

That's when Mickah stitched Deco a loaf, clean on the nose. It wasn't broken but snot and blood fell out of it at a fierce speed.

Outspan got Deco to hold his head back. Natalie dammed the flow with a couple of paper hankies.

—That's not soul either, Brother, Joey The Lips told Mickah.

—Probably not, said James.

—He shouldn't o' talken to yeh like tha'. ———I'm sorry, righ'.

—Tell Brother Deco that.

—I will in me ——

—Tell him.

———I'm sorry, righ'.

—Okay, said Deco. —Don't worry abou' it.

139

Deco's nose was under control.

Jimmy remembered the good news.

—There might be an A an' R man comin' to see us next week.

—Sent from The Lord, said Joey The Lips.

He held his palms out. Jimmy slapped them. Then Joey The Lips slapped Jimmy's palms.

—What's an A an' R man? Dean asked.

—I don't know wha' the A an' R stand for but they're talent scouts for record companies. They look at groups an' sign them up.

The Commitments whooped and smiled and laughed and hit each other. They were all very happy, even Deco.

—A and R means Artists and Repertory, said Joey The Lips.

—I thought so, said Mickah.

—Wha' label?

—A small one, said Jimmy.

—Aaaah! said Imelda. —A little one. ——That's lovely.

They laughed.

—Independent, said Jimmy.

—Good, said Dean.

—Wha' are they called?

—Eejit Records. ——They're Irish.

They liked the name.

—They'd want to be fuckin' eejits to want us.

—They're only comin' to see us, Jimmy warned.

—Don't worry, Jim, said Outspan. —We'll introduce them to Mickah.

—Good thinkin', said Mickah. —They'll fuckin' sign us alrigh'.

140

—Plenty o' lipstick next week, girls, said Jimmy.

—Fuck yourself, you, said Natalie.

* * *

Jimmy hoped the good news would keep The Commitments going. But he was worried. He was losing sleep. Having problems with them one at a time was bad, but now both Dean and Deco were getting uppity. And James was worried about his exams, and Mickah was a looper.

He didn't organize a rehearsal for the weekend, to give James time to study and to keep them away from each other so there'd be no rows before Wednesday.

Jimmy called to Dean's house on Friday. He wanted to talk to him and maybe even catch him in the act, listening to jazz.

Dean was watching Blankety Blank.

They went up to Dean's room. Jimmy eyed the wall for incriminating posters. Nothing; just an old one of Manchester United (Steve Coppell and Jimmy Greenhoff were in it) and one of Bruce Springsteen at Slane. But maybe Dean's wall hadn't caught up with Dean yet.

—Did yeh come on the bus? Dean asked Jimmy.

—I haven't gone home yet, said Jimmy. —I went for a few scoops with a few o' the lads ou' o' work. ——Bruxelles. ——D'yeh know it?

—Yeah.

—It's good. ——Some great lookin' judies.

—Yeah.

—Eh ——— I was thinkin' we could have a chat abou' the group.

—Wha' abou' it?

—Wha' d'yeh think of it?

—It's okay.

—Okay?

—Yeah. Okay. ——Why?

——How is it okay?

—Jaysis, Jimmy, I don't know. ——I like —— the lads, yeh know, Derek an' Outspan, an' James. An' Washin'ton D.C. An' Joey's taught me a lot, yeh know. ——I like the girls. They're better crack than most o' the young ones I know. ——It's good crack.

—Wha' abou' the music?

—It's okay, said Dean. ———It's good crack, yeh know. ——It's good.

—But?

—Ah, Jaysis, Jimmy. I don't want to sound snobby but —— fuck it, there's not much to it, is there? —— Just whack whack whack an' tha' fuckin' eejit, Cuffe, roarin' an' moanin' —— an' fuckin' gurglin'.

—Forget Cuffe. ———What's wrong with it?

Jimmy sounded hurt.

—Nothin'.

Dean was glad this was happening, although he was uncomfortable.

—Don't get me wrong, Jimmy. ———It's too easy. It doesn't stretch me. ——D'yeh know wha' I mean? Em, it was grand for a while, while I was learnin' to play. It's limitin', know wha' I mean? ———It's good crack but it's not art.

—Art!

—Well ——yeah.

—You've been listenin' to someone, haven't yeh?

—No.

142

—Watchin' Channel fuckin' 4. Art! Me arse!

—Slag away. Sticks an' stones.

—Art! said Jimmy. (Art was an option he'd done in school because there was no room for him in metal work and there was no way they could get him into home economics. That's what art was.) —Cop on, Dean, will yeh.

—Look, Jimmy, said Dean. ——I went through hell tryin' to learn to play the sax. I nearly jacked it in after every rehearsal. Now I can play it. An' I'm not stoppin'. I want to get better. ———It's art, Jimmy. It is. I express meself, with me sax instead of a brush, like. That's why I'm gettin' into the jazz. There's no rules. There's no walls, your man in The Observer said it ——

—I knew it! The Observer, I fuckin' knew it!

—Shut up a minute. Let me finish.

Dean was blushing. He'd let the bit about The Observer slip out. He hoped Jimmy wouldn't tell the rest of the lads.

—That's the difference between jazz an' soul. There's too many rules in soul. ——It's all walls.

—Joey called them corners.

—That's it, said Dean. —Dead on. ——Four corners an' you're back where yeh started from. D'yeh follow me?

—I suppose so, said Jimmy. —Are yeh goin' to leave?

—The Commitments?

—Yeah.

—No, Jaysis no. No way.

Jimmy was delighted with the way Dean answered him.

143

—How come? he said.

—It's good crack, said Dean. —It's good. The jazz is in me spare time. That's okay, isn't it?

—Yeah, sure.

—No, the soul's grand, Jimmy. It's good crack. It's just the artist in me likes to get ou' now an' again, yeh know.

—Yeah, righ'. I know wha' yeh mean. I'm the same way with me paintin'.

—Do you paint, Jimmy?

—I do in me bollix.

Dean was happy now. So he kept talking, to please Jimmy.

—No, I wouldn't want to leave The Commitments. It's great crack. The lads are great. ——You're doin' a good job too. An' ——Keep this to yourself now.

—Go on.

——I fancy Imelda a bit too, yeh know.

—Everyone fancies 'melda, Dean.

—She's great, isn't she?

—Oh, she is indeed. ——A grand young one. ——Wha' abou' Joey's ideas abou' soul bein' the people's music an' tha'?

—Don't get me wrong, said Dean. —Joey's great. ——He's full o' shi'e though. ——Isn't he?

—I suppose he is a bit now tha' yeh mention it. ——Brother Dean. ——But go easy on the solos though, righ'.

—Okay.

★ ★ ★

Now that Jimmy thought of it, Imelda might have

144

been holding The Commitments together. Derek fancied her, and Outspan fancied her. Deco fancied her. He was sure James fancied her. Now Dean fancied her too. He fancied her himself.

Imelda had soul.

* * *

There was no review in Hot Press. That was a disappointment. But they were in the Rhythm Guide.

 —Your Regular Beat . . .

 What's Happening In Residencies.

 Wednesdays.

 Carlow, Octopussys: The Plumbers.

 Cork, Sir Henrys: Asthmatic Hobbit Goes
  Boing.

 Dublin, Baggot: The Four Samurai.

 Dublin, Ivy Rooms: Autumn's Drizzle.

 Dublin, Miami Vice: The Commitments.

Jimmy cut it out and stuck it on his wall.

* * *

The Commitments all arrived on Wednesday. They all helped with the gear. They all looked well. Deco's hooter was back to normal.

 —Is he here yet? James asked.

He stood behind Jimmy. Jimmy was sitting at a table at the door, taking in the money.

 —Who?

 —The man from Eejit.

 —Not yet. I'd say he'll come though.

 —I sure as hell hope so, Massa Jimmy, said James.

145

—I'll have to piss off righ' after, okay. I've another oral tomorrow afternoon.

—Fair enough, said Jimmy. —Count tha' for us.

Hot Press arrived, with someone else.

—He's here, Jimmy told James. —Tell the others, will yeh.

—Goodie goodie, said James.

—Howyis, lads, said Jimmy.

—Hi there, said Hot Press. —The review'll be in the next issue, okay. We were out of space. A big ad, you know.

—No problem, said Jimmy.

—This is Dave I was telling you about last week, remember?

—Oh, yeah, said Jimmy. —Howyeh, Dave. —— Jimmy ———Rabbitte.

He shook Dave's hand.

—Hi, Jimmy, said Dave. —Maurice tells me your guys are good, yeah?

—He's righ' too, said Jimmy. —They have it alrigh'. ——Go on ahead in, lads. I'll be with yis in a minute. I'll just rob a few more punters.

Jimmy was shaking.

The Commitments were great. Everything was right. They looked great too. Each one of them was worth watching.

They started with Knock on Wood. Mickah was cheered every time he loafed the drum. Then they did I Thank You. Then Chain Gang, Reach Out — I'll Be There and then they slowed down with Tracks of My Tears. After that, What Becomes of the Broken Hearted. Then The Commitmentettes took over with Walking in the Rain, Stoned Love and Stop in the Name of Love.

146

Once the crowd knew that The Commitmentettes were finished they began to shout for Night Train.

They got it four songs later.

—ALL ABOARD, said Deco. —THE NIGH' TRAIN.

There was pushing. Someone fell, but was up quickly. Nothing serious happened. They swayed and bopped as Deco did the roll call of American cities.

The crowd was waiting, getting ready.

—AN' DON'T FORGET NEW ORLEANS — THE HOME O' THE BLUES ——

OH YEAH ——

WE'RE COMIN' HOME ——

All The Commitments could see now after the front rows was hands in the air, clapping, and a few women on boyfriends' backs. Outspan grinned. Derek laughed. This was great.

—THE NIGH' TRAIN —

CARRIES ME HOME ——

THE NIGH' TRAIN —

CARRIES ME HOME —

SHO' NUFF IT DOES ———

Jimmy looked at Dave from Eejit. He was smiling.

Deco and the girls chugged while The Commitments brought the train around for the home stretch.

Deco broke away from the girls.

He growled: —STARTIN' OFF IN CONNOLLY —

Screams, roars and whistles.

—MOVIN' ON OU' TO KILLESTER —

Everyone jumped in time, including Dave from Eejit. And Jimmy.

147

—HARMONSTOWN RAHENY —

AN' DON'T FORGET KILBARRACK —
THE HOME O' THE BLUES ——

HOWTH JUNCTION BAYSIDE —

GOIN' HOME —

THEN ON OU' TO SUTTON WHERE
THE SNOBBY BASTARDS LIVE —

OH YEAH ——

OH YEAH ——

The crowd sang with Deco.

—NIGH' TRAIN —

COMIN' HOME FROM THE BOOZER —

NIGH' TRAIN —

COMIN' HOME FROM THE COM-
MITMENTS —

NIGH' TRAIN —

GETTIN' SICK ON THE BLOKE BESIDE
YEH —

NIGH' TRAIN —

BUT IT DOESN'T MATTER COS HE'S
ASLEEP —

NIGH' TRAIN —

CARRIES ME HOME —

NIGH' TRAIN —

CARRIES ME HOME —

NIGH' TRAIN —

TO ME GAFF —

NIGH' TRAIN —

CARRIES ME HOME ——

OH YEAH ——

OH YEAH ——

Then The Commitments did it all over again. There
wasn't time for an encore but it didn't matter.

148

The Commitments were delighted with them-selves.

—You're professionals, Brothers and Sisters, said Joey The Lips. —You ooze soul.

—That's a lovely thing to say, Joey. You ooze soul too.
—I blush.

Dave from Eejit came over to the platform.

—Great show, said Dave.

—Thanks, pal, said Mickah.

—Very visual, said Dave.

—Didn't sound bad either, did it? said Mickah.

—It sounded great, said Dave. ———Ladies, wonderful. Amazing.

—Thanks very much, said Natalie.

—Yeah, said Bernie, —thanks.

—See now, said Natalie. —We're wonderful.

—Amaaazing, said Imelda.

Dave went over to Jimmy.

—Can we talk, em?

—Jimmy.

—Jimmy, right. Can we talk? Over here, yeah?

They went into a far corner. Hot Press came with them.

—Did yeh like tha', Dave? Jimmy asked.

—Great, terrific. ———Great.

—They're not bad at all, sure they're not, Dave? said Jimmy. —They need a bit o' polishin' maybe.

—No, no, said Dave. —That'd ruin them. Leave them as they are. Raw, you know.

—Fair enough. Wha'ever yeh say. You're the expert.

—The senior citizen. The trumpet, yeah? He's a terrific idea.

149

—That's Joey The Lips Fagan.

—Yeah.

—He played with James Brown.

—Right.

—Among others.

—The ladies too. ——Great visuals.

Jimmy nearly laughed. He hid behind his glass. Then he asked Dave a question.

——Would yeh be interested in us, Dave?

—Yeah, right. Definitely.

Jimmy held his glass to his chest. He knew it would rattle if he put it on the table.

Dave continued.

—We release singles only. At the moment. We're small, and happy that way, yeah? We're not in it for the lucre, yeah? You heard the Reality Margins single? Trigger Married Silver and Now They're Making Ponies? From the Fanning session?

Jimmy lied.

—Yeah. ——It was very good.

—That was Eejit. ——It didn't get the airplay. They were scared of it, you know. ——We sign bands for one single, yeah? No fee, sorry. We pay for the studio time so long as it's not more than a day, and the producer. We do the package. A good picture cover. You've seen the label?

—Yeah, said Jimmy.

He wasn't lying this time.

—It's good ——very nice.

Hot Press spoke. —Dave set up Eejit as a springboard for new bands. The Eejit record is meant to be the first step on the ladder. The idea is that the major labels hear it and if they like you they sign you.

150

The Eejit single is to help you get a proper contract. It gives you a voice.

—That's right, said Dave.

—Tha' sounds fair enough, said Jimmy. —That'd be great. Has it worked so far?

—Yes and no, yeah? said Dave. —Reality Margins are before their time.

Hot Press laughed.

Dave explained.

—My little brother plays percussion for Reality Margins, yeah? But you know The Baby Docs?

—Yeah. ——Bitin' the Pillow. ——Yeah, it's good, tha'.

—CBS and Rough Trade are sniffing there, said Dave.

—That's good, said Jimmy. —I hope it works ou' okay for them now.

—So, Jimmy, said Dave. —Tell me. ——Would The Commitments be interested in recording Night Train for us?

—I'd say they would, yeah, said Jimmy. (And to himself: —Yeh fuckin' budgie, yeh!)

—You don't know for sure?

—We're a democratic group, Dave, said Jimmy. — Soul is democracy.

—Right, said Dave. —We could put that on the sleeve.

—Good thinkin'.

—I see a double A-side, said Dave. —Side A, the studio Night Train. The other side A, the live Night Train.

—I like it, said Hot Press.

—I'd buy tha', said Jimmy.

151

—It'd get the airplay, said Dave. —It'd sell. It'd chart, yeah? It's good, unspoilt roots stuff, you know. ——Pure. ——And very fuckin' funny.

Jimmy washed his giggles back with the last of his pint.

——Would we have to pay you annythin', Dave? he asked.

—No, said Dave. —It's cool. ——We're funded by the Department of Labour, yeah? Youth employment, yeah? They pay me. Any profit goes back into Eejit.

—Go 'way! said Jimmy. —That's grand.

—I suppose I'm just a hippy, you know, said Dave. —And my parents are rich. ——Are The Commitments on the dole?

——Some o' them.

—That's good, said Dave. —The Department will like that.

Hot Press laughed.

—We'd have to sign somethin', wouldn't we? said Jimmy.

—Right, yeah. A simple, one-off contract, yeah?

—We could do tha' annytime.

—Right.

—Yeh don't have one on yeh, I suppose?

—Tomorrow.

—Okay, righ'. ——I'll see if I can talk the group into it. Will we have to meet annyone?

—No.

—No one from Eejit?

—I'm Eejit.

Hot Press laughed again.

—Just yourself?

—Just myself, said Dave.

152

He pretended to type.

—I'm even the secretary, yeah?

—Fair play to yeh, Dave, said Jimmy.

Jimmy went to the door with them. They said their goodbyes and arranged to meet the next night in The Bailey.

Jimmy took some deep breaths.

That was perfect. The Commitments wouldn't be tied to a little gobshite label run by hippies. Just the one single (Night Train would be a big hit in Dublin) and the big boys would be queuing up for The Commitments, readies in hand. Jimmy wondered if they should wait a bit before they gave up their jobs.

Jimmy took one more long breath, clapped his hands, rubbed them, and went back inside to tell The Commitments.

But they didn't exist any more. Somewhere in the quarter of an hour Jimmy had been negotiating with Dave from Eejit, The Commitments had broken up.

Outspan and Derek were the only ones still at the platform. The rest were gone.

Jimmy leaned against the wall.

——Wha'?

—They all fucked off, said Outspan.

He was explaining how it had happened.

—Why?

—I'm not sure, said Outspan. —It was over before I copped on tha' ann'thin, was happenin'. ——Do you know, Derek?

—I think it was when Deco seen Joey kissin' 'melda.

—Imelda?

—Yeah.

153

—Wha' abou' Bernie?

—She didn't seem to mind.

—For fuck sake! said Jimmy. ——Real kissin', like?

—Oh yeah, said Derek. —They were warin' alrigh'. Over where you are.

—I seen tha' bit alrigh' said Outspan.

He shook his head.

—Nearly puked me ring.

—Then Deco said he was sick o' this, said Derek, —an' he pulled Joey away from her, righ'. An' he called 'melda a prick teaser. An' tha' wasn't on cos she isn't, so I went to give him a boot, righ'. But then Deco had a go at Joey. I think he fancied 'melda, d'yeh know tha'? ——He gave Joey a dig. Hurt him. Then Mickah went for Deco. He got him a few slaps an' Deco ran ou' an' he said The Commitments could fuck off an' Mickah went after him.

—How come I didn't see annythin'? Jimmy asked.

—It happened very fuckin' fast, said Outspan. —I didn't see ann'thin' either an' I was here, sure.

—Where's James?

—He had to go, remember?

—That's righ'. ——Dean?

—Dean took it very badly, Jim, said Derek.

—I heard this bit, said Outspan. —He ——Listen to this now. ——He said he was fucked if he was goin' to waste his time jammin' — Jammin'! — jammin' with a shower o' wankers tha' couldn't play their instruments properly. ——Tha' wasn't on. —— I gave him a dig. An' he fucked off. I think he was cryin'. ——Spa!

——Fuckin' great, said Jimmy.

—D'yeh know wha'? said Derek. —I think Dean

154

fancies 'melda too. It's a gas really when yeh think abou'
it.

—It's a fuckin' scream, said Jimmy. —Where's
Joey?

—He went to the hospital. He thinks his nose is
broke. The girls went with him but I don't think he
wanted them to. He was tryin' to get away from them.
They had to run after him.

Jimmy sat down on the platform.

Derek continued.

—It's funny. ——I think Joey was the oney one of
us tha' didn't fancy Imelda an' he's the oney one of us
tha' got off with her. Fuckin' gas really, isn't it?

Jimmy said nothing for a while. He looked at the
ground. Outspan and Derek reckoned that he was
thinking, thinking things out.

Then he spoke. —Fuck yis annyway. ——Fuck the
lot o' yis.

—We didn't do ann'thin'! said Outspan.

——Fuck yis, said Jimmy, quietly. ——Yis bastards.

The head barman came out of the room behind the
bar.

—Why aren't yis gone? he shouted.

—Most of us are gone, pal, said Outspan.

—Fuck yis, said Jimmy to the floor. —Just ——

He swept his hand over his knee.

—Fuck yis.

—Come on, said the head barman.

—Hang on a sec, said Derek.

He bent down to Jimmy.

—Sorry 'bou' tha', Jimmy, he said.

He put his hand on Jimmy's shoulder.

—-Still. ——-It was good while it lasted, wasn't it?
—Ah fuck off! said Jimmy.
That sort of talk gave Jimmy the pip.

* * *

Jimmy phoned Joey The Lips about a week after The Commitments broke up.

He hadn't tried to get them together again. He hadn't wanted to. They were fuckin' saps. He'd watched telly all week. It wasn't too bad. He'd gone for a few scoops with the lads from work on the Friday. That was his week.

He hadn't gone into The Bailey to meet Dave from Eejit.

He hadn't played any soul.

Now, a week after, he thought he was over it. He'd nearly cried when he was in bed that night. He'd have loved to have seen that Commitments single, with them on the cover, and maybe a video for Anything Goes. But now he was okay. They were tossers. So was Dave from Eejit. He had better things to do with his life.

But he was phoning Joey The Lips, just to say cheerio, and good luck, because Joey The Lips wasn't like the others. Joey The Lips was different. He'd taught them all a thing or two.

Joey The Lips answered.

—The Fagan household.

—Joey? ——Howyeh. This is Jimmy.

—Jimmy! My main man. How are you, Brother?

—Grand. How's your nose?

—It's still hanging on in there.

156

—Tha' was a fuckin' terrible thing for Deco to do.

—Forget it, forget it. ——When I was leaving the hospital they were bringing Brother Declan in.

—Wha'?

—On a stretcher.

—Go 'way! ——Funny. I haven't seen him since. I'd forgot he works where I work.

—Have you seen the other Brothers and Sisters?

—No way. I don't want to.

—Hmm. ——A pity.

——Wha' are yeh goin' to do now?

—America calls, Brother. I'm going back. Maybe soul isn't right for Ireland. So I'm not right. I'm going back to the soul.

—When?

—The day after tomorrow. Joe Tex called me. You've heard Joe Tex?

—I've heard the name alrigh'. ——Hang on. He had a hit there. Ain't Gonna Bump No More with No Big Fat Woman.

—Correct. ——Joe wants me to tour with him again.

—Fair play to yeh. ——Annyway, Joey, I phoned yeh to thank yeh for everythin', yeh know. ——So ——thanks.

—Oh, I blush. Thank The Lord, not me.

—You thank him for me, okay?

—I will do. ——Will you continue the good work, Jimmy?

—No way. I've learnt me lesson.

————Hang on one minute.

—Okay.

Joey The Lips was back.

157

—Howyeh, said Jimmy.

—Listen to this. ——O sing into the Lord, a new song, for he hath done marvellous things. Make a joyful noise unto the Lord, all the earth make a loud noise, and rejoice, and song praise. ——Psalm Number 98, Brother Jimmy.

—Fuck off, Joey. Good luck.

Jimmy was in the kitchen filling the kettle when he remembered something, something he'd read a while back. Joe Tex died in 1982.

* * *

Jimmy met Imelda about a week after that. She had her sister's baby with her. Jimmy cutchie–cutchie–cooed it. It stared out at him.

—Is it a young one or a young fella?

—A young fella. ——Eddie. He's a little fucker, so he is. He's always cryin'. Aren't yeh a little fucker, Eddie?

Eddie belched.

—No manners, he hasn't. ——Wha' have yeh been doin' with yourself since an'annyway? Imelda asked Jimmy.

—Nothin'. ——Nothin' much.

—Have yeh seen anny o' the others?

—No.

—Have yeh seen Joey?

—Have YOU not? said Jimmy. —He's gone back to America.

—Has he? The little fucker.

—Wha'?

—He never said bye bye or ann'thin'.

158

Jimmy had decided not to mention Joe Tex to anyone.

—He's tourin' again. With The Impressions, I think he said.

—That's lovely, for some. ———D'yeh know wha', Jimmy? ——Don't tell annyone this now.

Jimmy said nothing.

—Promise not to tell.

—I promise, said Jimmy.

—I think Joey left because of us.

—Wha' d'yeh mean?

—Me an' Bernie an' Nat'lie.

—Because yis all got off with him, d'yeh mean?

—Yeah. Sort of. ——He was scared of us.

—D'yeh reckon? ———D'yeh mind if I ask? said Jimmy. —How come yis all got off with him?

—Ah, we were messin', yeh know. We did not like him but. It wasn't just messin'. ——It became a sort of joke between us. To see if we could all get off with him.

—Lucky Joey, wha'.

—Wha'? ——oh yeah.

She laughed a bit.

—I suppose he was really. ——The three of us.

She laughed again.

—I think I went a bit too far though.

—How, like?

—I told him I thought I was pregnint.

—GOOD JAYSIS!

Jimmy roared laughing.

—Yeh fuckin' didn't!

—I did, Jimmy. ———Me others were late.

Jimmy fought back a redner.

159

—How long?

—A few days, a week nearly.

—Ah Jaysis! Imelda! ——Poor Joey.

He laughed again.

—I didn't really think I was pregnant. I shouldn't o' done it. I just wanted to see wha' he'd do.

—He fucked off to America.

—I know, said Imelda. —The shi'e.

Jimmy giggled. So did Imelda.

—He hadn't much, willpower, d'yeh know wha' I mean? said Imelda. —He was a bit of a tramp, Joey was.

They both laughed.

—Come 'ere, said Imelda. —If you're startin' another group let us be in it, will yeh? It was brilliant crack.

—I won't be, said Jimmy.

—Sonya, Tanya an' Sofia, said Imelda. —It was fuckin' brilliant.

* * *

—Righ', said Jimmy. —Are yis righ'?

—Fire away, Jimmy, said Mickah.

Outspan and Derek were sitting beside him on the bunk.

—This is The Byrds, righ', said Jimmy. —I'll Feel a Whole Lot Better.

He let the needle down and sat on the back of his legs between the speakers.

There was a bit of a crackle (it was a second-hand album), then a guitar jangled and then they were

160

surrounded by jangling guitars. **They'd no time to get ready.**

   —THE REASON WHY — EE ——
     OH I CAN'T STAY — AY — Y ——
     I HAVE TO LET YOU GO BAY — AYBE
——

     AND RIGHT AWAY — AY — Y ——
     AFTER ALL YOU DID ————
     I CAN'T STAY OH — H — H — ON —
     AND I'LL PROBABLY —

Two high-pitched men joined in here.

   —FEEL A WHOLE LOT BETTER —
         WHEN YOU'RE GOH — ON —

The lads weren't bouncing up and down on the bunk for this music. They were throwing their heads and chests out and back, out and back. Their feet didn't tap: they slammed. Outspan strummed the air.

   —BABY FOR A LONG TIME —

The other Byrds repeated the line.

   —BABY FOR A LONG TIME —
   —YOU HAD ME BELIE — IE — IEVE —

The others: —YOU HAD ME BELIEVE —

   —THAT YOUR LOVE WAS ALL MI — I — I
— INE —

The others: — YOUR LOVE WAS ALL MINE
—

   —AND THAT'S THE WAY IT WOULD BE
———— EE — EE —

The others: —LAA —
        AAH —
          AAH —
            AAAAAH ————

Thirty seconds into the song the lads wanted to be

161

The Byrds. They'd been demolished by the rip-roaring guitars and Gene Clark's manly whinge. It was sweet and rough at the same time. The guitars raced each other.

It was the best they'd ever heard. They didn't just hear it either. They were in its way. It went through them. Man's music.

—AFTER WHAT YOU DI — I — ID —

The other Byrds: —AFTER WHAT YOU DID —

—I CAN'T STAY ON — OH — ON —

The others: —I CAN'T STAY ON —

All The Byrds: —AND I'LL PROBABLY —

                         FEEL   A   WHOLE   LOT

BETTER —

    WHEN YOU'RE GOH — ON ——

    OH WHEN YOU'RE GOH — ON ——

    OH WHEN YOU'RE GOH — ON ——

    OH WHEN YOU'RE GOH — ON ——

More jangling guitars winding down and it was over.

Jimmy got the needle up quickly. The next track, The Bells of Rhymney, was a piece of hippy shite and he didn't want the lads to hear it.

—Tha' was fuckin' rapid, said Outspan. —Play it again, Jimmy.

—Deadly, wasn't it? said Derek.

—Listen to this, said Mickah.

—BABY FOR A LON TAM ——

    YEH HAD ME BEL — EE — EE — EE — EVE —

—My Jaysis, Mickah! ——— Fair play to yeh.

—We've a singer, said Jimmy.

—An' you could play the drums, Jimmy, said Derek.

—Yeah, said Outspan. —Just the four of us, wha'. No pricks.

—Is tha' wha' we want? Jimmy asked them.

That was what they wanted.

—Bass, guitar, drums an' Mickah, said Derek. — Rapid.

—Play it again, said Outspan.

—Hang on, said Jimmy. —Could you play like tha'?

—No problem to me, said Outspan.

—The bass sounds easier than for soul, said Derek.

—We'll need two guitars.

—We will in our arses, said Outspan. —I'll use both hands.

—Good thinkin'.

—Wha' abou' James?

—We'll let him in when he's a doctor, said Mickah. —Tha' comes first.

—Tha' won't be for ages.

Jimmy spoke. —He'll be a doctor abou' the same time we're puttin' our third album together. An' we'll need a gentler sound, righ', a new direction, like, after the first two cos they'll be real country-punk albums. James' piano will fit in nicely then.

—That's grand. ———Will we tell him?

—No. We'll keep it as a surprise for him.

—Play it again, said Outspan.

—Wha' abou' the girls? said Derek.

—Wha' abou' them?

—Will we let them in?

—Ah, yeah, said Outspan. —The girls are sound.

163

—I know, said Mickah. —They could wear tha'
Dolly Parton sort o' clobber. Yeh know, the frilly bits
on the elbows an' tha' sort o' shi'e.

—Do we want the girls? Jimmy asked.

They did.

—They could give us a rest, said Derek. —They
could sing a few slowies. For the oul' ones.

—An' the young ones.

—That's the lot though, righ', said Jimmy. —No
fuckin' politics this time either. ———But, yeh know,
Joey said when he left tha' he didn't think soul was
righ' for Ireland. This stuff is though. You've got to
remember tha' half the country is fuckin' farmers. This
is the type o' stuff they all listen to. ———Only they
listen to it at the wrong speed.

—We'll put them righ' though, wha'. Play it again,
Jimmy, will yeh.

—Will we have names? Derek asked.

—Ah Jaysis, no, said Jimmy. —Not tha' shi'e again.
This is different.

Outspan agreed with him.

—Would yis mind, said Mickah, —if I had a bit of
a name?

—Wha'?

—Tex.

They laughed. They liked it.

—Tex Wallace. ———It sounds righ', doesn't it? said
Mickah.

Jimmy was putting the needle down when he
thought of something else.

—Oh yeah, he said. —We don't have a name. ———
Anny ideas?

—Well, said Derek. —Yeh know the way they're

The Byrds an' Bird is another name for a girl, righ'?

——Couldn't we be The Brassers?

It was a great name.

—Dublin country, said Jimmy. —That's fuckin' perfect. The Brassers. ———We're a Dublin country group.

—That's an excellent name, Derek, said Outspan.

—Ah ———I just thought of it, yeh know.

Jimmy put the needle back on its stand.

—Another thing I forgot to tell yis. ——I was in touch with your man, Dave, from Eejit Records, remember? I asked him would he be interested in a country-punk version o' Nigh' Train, an' he said he migh' be.

—That's brilliant, said Derek.

—Hang on, said Mickah.

—STARTIN' OU' IN MULLINGAR

   MOVIN' ON OU' TO KINNEGAD ——

Somethin' like tha'?

—That's very good, said Jimmy.

They laughed.

—That's very good, alrigh', said Outspan. —I like tha'. Fair play.

Jimmy had the needle ready.

—Righ', lads, give us a month an' this'll be us.

He let the needle down.

—Deadly, said Derek.

* * *